MAGIC OF THIEVES

C. Greenwood

A BEGINNING

T HE BRISK AUTUMN WIND PLAYS through my
hair and tugs at my clothes impatiently,
as if trying to pull me down the forest trail
more quickly. Each new gust sends a storm of red
and ocher leaves showering to the earth to crunch
beneath my boots as I follow a well-remembered
path to a better remembered destination, one
that has been my home almost longer than I can
remember. One that will be my home no more
after today.

Unwilling to explore the feelings accompanying
that realization, I jerk my thoughts quickly in a
safer direction. It's surprisingly easy to feel hopeful
right now, despite the previous day's events. The
birds are noisy in the trees overhead and the
sun is rising in the sky to warm my back. Or
possibly that reassuring warmth is radiating from
something less dependable than the sun – the bow
slung across my back. The bow often grows warm,
glowing with an eerie light for no apparent reason.
I'm still not used to that. I'm not used to a great
many things, not the least of which is the plan
before me and all that led me to it.

As my steps draw me nearer to Red Rock camp, I find my memories drifting to an area less familiar, to a time and place almost forgotten, and to a voice lost to me many years ago ...

CHAPTER ONE

"**H**URRY, LITTLE ONE. WE MUST be ready as soon as Da pulls the cart up to the door." Mama's voice was tense and her hands were busy as she spoke, shoving food and provisions into a bag.

"I'm trying, Mama," I whined. "But I cannot find my boots."

"Never mind. There's no more time," she said, snatching a woolen scarf from a peg on the wall and kneeling to wind it around my head and shoulders. I couldn't understand the reason behind the tight lines around her mouth or the dread filling her eyes.

She said, "You'll be riding in the cart, so we'll just wrap your feet up snug in a blanket. Come now, quickly."

She grabbed my thin shoulders and pushed me toward the door. Her grip dug painfully into my flesh and I gave a little squeal of protest, but she appeared not to hear it.

I was amazed at being permitted to go outdoors with bare feet in the dead of winter, something that had never happened according to my short memory. I still wore my sleeping gown beneath my cloak, and my silver-white hair remained matted and uncombed.

Mama threw open the door and an icy blast of wind slapped me in the face, cutting through my clothing. I peered out through the torrential sleet and into the dim world ahead. It was not yet light out, but I could just see far enough ahead to make out Da pulling the cart into the yard, our old nag hitched to the front.

Grabbing my wrist, Mama dragged me out the door and down the front step, moving with surprising strength for a woman so small. My naked feet barely touched the frozen ground but when they did the cold of the sleet-spattered mud made me cringe, so I ran as fast as my short legs could carry me across the yard.

A shrill scream erupted suddenly in the distance. Carried on the wind, it echoed across the valley, rising over the gale of the storm.

Fear shot up my spine as Mama froze for a moment, looking off toward the hills ringing our farm. A little village lay just over the near rise, but it was impossible to see beneath the darkness and the thick veil of the blizzard.

Spurred by the scream and the series of chilling cries that followed, Mama took to her heels again. I stumbled over the frozen earth and she grabbed me up in her slender arms, carrying me the rest of the way to the cart. I could feel her heart thudding against my ear as she ran, her breath rasping in and out as she stumbled to a halt alongside the wagon.

Then I was passed into Da's strong arms and lifted upward.

"They're coming!" Mama had to shout at him to be heard over the wind. "They're in the village!"

"I heard." Da sounded unrushed. His eyes met hers over the top of my head and she seemed to grow calmer beneath his steady gaze.

She said, "We've no chance of outrunning the soldiers. Not in a cart."

"Not together," he agreed. "But with the weight of only two you might make it."

"Habon, what are you saying?"

Da didn't answer immediately, settling me down quickly in the bed of the cart and giving me a reassuring pat on the head.

"I want you to make for Borlan's farm on the other side of the ridge," he told Mama. "Borlan's a magickless, but he's a good neighbor and I believe he'll hide you from the Praetor's Fists. At any rate, he's your only chance."

"I won't go without you," she insisted.

Da turned his back to her, making a hasty check of the nag's harness. "You must, Ada. You understand what has to be done for the sake of the child. Quickly now, get into the cart."

Another unexpected cry rent the air—not the terrified scream of a distant villager this time, but a ferocious howl of bloodlust. The shout was swiftly echoed by a host of others, each sounding closer than the last.

I fixed my eyes on the dark line of the ridge in the distance, knowing at any moment something terrible was going to crest the rise, even if I couldn't guess what. I heard Mama choke on a sob, was aware of her falling into Da's arms, but couldn't tear my gaze from the hill. A handful of shadowy figures on horseback suddenly vaulted over the rise and into view. Then, what looked like an entire army was pouring down the hillside like a flood, aimed directly at us.

The scene wasn't lost on Mama and Da.

"You've been a good husband to me," she said quickly. "And a good father to our daughter."

He nodded wordlessly and bent his head to hers in a swift kiss.

Then, without another word, he was gone, a tall shadow disappearing into the falling sleet.

I had no time to comprehend what was happening. Mama scrambled into the cart ahead of me and took up the reins. I looked back over my shoulder and saw the descending horde of horsemen riding into our farmyard. One instant they filled my vision, a black tide surging toward us, the next, a lone shape stepped into their path. My Da made a strange figure, standing alone before the fierce inflowing host, a wheat scythe gripped in his hand.

Our cart lurched forward, and I was slung roughly against the back as we bumped along, picking up speed. I glanced behind us in time to see the dark figure that was my Da disappearing beneath the thundering hooves of the first horsemen.

"Da!" I screeched.

I threw myself over the side of the moving cart, hitting the ground with a force that drove the breath from my lungs and sent a jolt of agony through my body. I rolled a short distance in the mud. For a brief eternity, I couldn't breathe, couldn't move. Cold sleet hailed down on my upturned face. I labored to draw an aching breath and then was sucking in the air in great gulps, choking on the freezing rain that found its way down my nose and into my mouth.

Footsteps pounded toward me. Suddenly, Mama was there, kneeling in the mud beside me, lifting me gently off my back and tucking my head under her dry cloak. I clung to her waist, shivering against her warmth, and breathed in the heavy scent of soggy wool. Then I became aware of the rumbling of hooves, signaling the approach of many horses. Safety disappeared as the world came rushing in on me again.

Mama quickly pushed me back from her and set me on my feet. I tried to crawl into her lap again, but she held me firmly at arm's length.

I squinted through the downpour and made out the shapes of the horsemen bearing down on us, their scarlet cloaks flaring out behind them, the beating of their horses' hooves drowning out the thunder of the skies.

Mama's hands were clumsy, her face slick with rain so I couldn't tell if she was weeping or if I imagined it. Taking my head in her hands, she put her forehead against mine until I could see nothing but her face. Her eyes were wide, her mouth tight. Strands of wet hair, whiter than pure snow, clung to her face and neck.

She shouted over the roar of the battering wind, "I need you to be brave for me! You must hold tight to what I'm about to give you and never lose it, for if all else fails, it may protect you."

Fumbling inside her cloak, she withdrew something that she pressed hastily into my hand. It was too dark to make out what it was, but the object was cold and hard like metal with ridged edges that cut into my palm when she closed my fingers tight around it.

"Take this and go to Master Borlan. You must run very fast until you can run no more, and then you must hide. Do you understand?"

Before I could answer, she pushed me roughly away from her and I reeled forward.

"Go now!" she commanded. "Hurry!"

I hesitated, every instinct telling me to disobey the incomprehensible order and cling to my one source of safety.

But she was already turning her back on me to face the approaching horses with arms outspread, as if she could hold back the tide of darkness. Blue sparks of magic appeared, sizzling at her fingertips.

As the nearest horsemen advanced, bright bolts

shot from Mama's hands, striking the ground at their feet. The earth erupted as if hit by lightning and chunks of mud flew through the air, spraying in every direction. Horses reared and shrieked, flailing their hooves. There were shouts from the men who fought to regain control of their mounts and several riders were thrown to the ground, but others barreled on.

Terror seized me at the sight of them closing in and, unthinkingly, I turned and fled. When next I looked back, it was to see the lead rider bearing down on Mama's slight figure. She stood firm, blue lightning crackling in her hands, but this time she didn't cast her magic swiftly enough. I saw the horseman's thick arm, holding a length of steel, sweep toward her in a single, smooth motion and she crumpled to the mud like a broken doll.

I felt nothing. No anguish, no horror. Senses overwhelmed, I ran like a wild creature to outpace my pursuers, until I made the shelter of the thick trees at the edge of the farmyard. Plunging into their depths, I was whipped by sharp branches and tripped by saplings and fallen logs looming out of nowhere. The darkness was so complete I couldn't tell where I was going.

One moment I was stumbling blindly through the undergrowth, the next, my feet tangled in a thick tree root and I fell headlong into an overgrown pile of brush. Thorny leaves pricked my hands and face, immediately setting my skin tingling with the mild toxin they secreted. I struggled to fight my way free of the mass, succeeding only in gathering more injuries and tangling my hair among the branches.

In the distance, I heard a heavy crashing sound as something, or *several* somethings, entered the stand of trees and attempted to force their way through the brush. At the sounds of jangling harness and stamping horses I lay motionless, pain and discomfort forgotten. Blood rushed in my ears and my heart beat an unsteady rhythm. The harshness of my breathing sounded louder than the noise of the approaching horsemen, and I wondered if my enemies could hear it, for they moved closer with every second.

Heavy blundering noises and men's muttered curses told me the darkness and density of the forest impeded their progress.

A voice commanded, "Dismount before the horses stumble. They can't see where they're going in this plague-cursed darkness."

Hearing the sounds of shifting armor and that of many feet thudding to the ground, I trembled and burrowed deeper into my thorny hiding place, ignoring the pain as the needly leaves pierced my skin. My lanced hands and face were growing strangely numb.

The startling crack of a stick underfoot alerted me that at least one of my pursuers stood mere paces from me. I strained to see him but could make out nothing, not so much as a moving shadow in the darkness. I squeezed my fingers tight around the round metal trinket Mama had thrust into my hand and pressed myself flatter to the ground, the movement rustling the leaves around me.

The stranger's deep voice was terrifyingly near. "Is that you I hear, little witch? Hiding from old Logart, are ye?"

His chuckle was followed by an unfamiliar whisper, like the sound of drawn steel.

As he stamped at the surrounding shrubbery, I wrapped my arms around my head and willed myself to sink into the earth or to turn into a pebble or an insect, anything beneath notice. To my dismay, I remained a solid human being.

The frightening stranger spoke as if to himself, but his voice was loud enough that I knew he meant me to hear. "They say you magickers can summon fire and wind at will," he said. "And that you can speak to the dead and call wild beasts to defend ye. Well, old Logart doesn't believe everything he hears. But he's a loyal Praetor's man and if the Praetor wants his lands cleansed of your kind, than cleansed they'll be."

His foot sank into the thorny brush beside me, his shiny black boot resting next to my hand. A finger's breadth farther and he would be crushing my fingers. He had but to look down to see me huddled at his feet.

Terrified, I did something I had never done before, something Mama told me it would be years before I could do. I reached inward, seizing hold of the tiny new flame of magic just beginning to flicker within me, and stoked that fitful fire to a roar. Remembering how Mama had looked crumpling lifeless to the ground, I fed grief and outrage into the potent mixture I was creating.

Even as I concentrated on the magic I was forming, a vague, unsought awareness of my enemy's cold weariness filtered through my senses. Startled by this unfamiliar consciousness of another being, I almost dropped my hold on the magic. Quickly, I released the weapon I had formed, casting it from me and into the path of my enemy.

My magic slammed into him and, with a muffled shriek, he stumbled backward, dropping his sword. I heard him collapse to the ground, then there was no sound but the rattling, wheezing noises of his struggle for breath as the magic fastened itself to his throat. I lay still and waited until the sounds of his choking ceased.

I could still hear the others out there, crashing through the wet underbrush, but I felt too drained to move. My body was numb, disconnected from my mind, as I lay listening to my heartbeat and feeling drops of sweat form, despite the cold, and trickle down my ribs.

A distant shout went up. "Captain! We've caught up to the cart, sir, but there's no one else in it. Or if there were others, they've jumped out and got a headstart on us."

There followed some noisy conferring about whether to continue pursuing "the child" or to concentrate their search on the other possible escapees. I heard my nonexistent companions declared a higher priority than I, and soon the footsteps of my enemies receded into the distance.

Too exhausted to feel relief or to think of using this opportunity to run, I closed my eyes and groped after that strength-giving fire within, but it had deserted me.

The events that followed were a hazy blur to me. I slept among the thorny leaves for what seemed like days, but might only have been hours, until the neighbor my Da had trusted came to discover what had become of our homestead. Master Borlan found me among the trees and carried me back to his home. I recovered from the effects of the thorn bush's toxin and Master Borlan's family kept me hidden in a cellar beneath their farmhouse for weeks, so I survived the cruel times that destroyed most of the magickers in the province.

I leaned all this when it was later recounted by Master Borlan, but I couldn't have been above six years old and my memory holds little record of that dangerous time. I don't recall the fear I must have felt cowering in the dark of the cellar or the fading fever and partial paralysis as the toxin worked its way out of my body. I have no memory of the fearful, whispered conversations that must have taken place over my head, nor could I have had any comprehension of the grave risk Da's friend took upon himself and his family in protecting me from the soldiers determined to wipe out my people.

But of this I must have been aware. My future was uncertain and I was very much alone.

CHAPTER TWO

THE THREADS OF MY MEMORY are taken up again on a damp day in late winter, when I found myself waiting alongside a muddy road cutting past the far side of Master Borlan's farm. Not too great a time could have passed since the night my parents were murdered because there was still a bone-deep chill in the air and the dreary weather remained.

I wore clean clothing that must have come from one of Master Borlan's daughters and was shod in a sturdy pair of boots that felt too tight around my toes, but were infinitely better than standing on the cold ground. My old cloak had been washed and mended. Only from these details can I surmise what must have been the attitude of Master Borlan's wife toward me. She had bundled me efficiently against the wet and cold, and I don't recall that I felt afraid or ill treated, only curious, as I stood at Master Borlan's side and stared up at the peddler atop the rickety wagon drawing to a halt before us.

"What kept you, man?" Master Borlan demanded. "The arrangements were made for dawn and we've been waiting half the morning. I was near to giving up and going back home."

The elderly wagon driver showed no remorse. "On a day like this, you can thank the fates I came at all," he said. "Bad weather for traveling." He cast an eye toward the cloudy skies and the light drizzle raining steadily down.

The gray mare hitched to the front of the wagon curved her neck around to regard us with a long, lazy stare mirroring that of her master.

"You've the money?" the old peddler questioned, extending an upturned palm.

He had a bony hand, which shook slightly, though whether from age or overindulgence in the cheap spirits he reeked of, it was impossible to tell. When Master Borlan dug into his purse and deposited a few shiny coins in the peddler's hand, the old man snatched the money greedily and pocketed it with haste.

Only then did he show any curiosity toward me. The brim of his hat was bent downward beneath the weight of the rainwater collected atop it and he had to tilt his head back to view me from beneath.

"This is the child, then?" he asked, his gaze critical. "Looks pale and skinny to me. You're sure she hasn't been touched by the plague?"

"The child is healthy enough," Master Borlan said evenly, "and she had better be still when she arrives in the next province. I'm entrusting her to your safekeeping."

"Aye, I'll look after her right enough," the

peddler snapped defensively. "Gave my word, didn't I? But it's a powerful risk you're asking of me. If I'm caught smuggling a young magicker over the border—"

"You've been well paid for your risk," Master Borlan interrupted. "Plenty of children around here have the silver hair and pale skin of Skeltai ancestry, so no one should give this one a second look. Just deposit her in a safe magicker settlement in Cros and your duty will be discharged."

The peddler grunted reluctant agreement.

Master Borlan lifted me up, setting me on the slippery wooden seat beside the old man, and tugging the hood of my cloak down to shield my head from the rain. It was too late for that. My hair was already slicked to my skull and I was shivering like a wet pup.

Master Borlan said to me, "You understand what is happening, child? You're being taken to a place where you can be with more of your kind, a place where you'll be safe from the Praetor's soldiers. All you must do is conceal your magic until you arrive there."

I nodded but was suddenly afraid at the prospect of leaving this last familiar face behind me.

"Why don't you take me there?" I asked.

He looked uncomfortable and it came to me in a flash that this large, strong man was afraid. Afraid the red-cloaked horsemen would come and murder him as they had my family and the other magickers in our village. Even now, none of us were safe.

A shadow seemed to fall over the day, and I shuddered beneath my cloak.

Observing the motion, Master Borlan squeezed my shoulder with a heavy, work-roughened hand. "You'll be all right, girl," he said briskly, but he wouldn't meet my eyes as he pressed something cold into my hand. "You were holding this the night…"

I knew he wanted to say the night Mama and Da died.

For the first time, I really looked at the object my mother had given me on that last terrible parting. It was a big, fine looking brooch of the type a man might use to fasten his clothing and was made of hammered metal, inlaid with copper and amber colored stones.

Master Borlan said, "You spoke of your mother wanting you to keep it with you, so here it is. Only pin it to the inside of your waistband, where it won't be lost or seen. I don't know how your mother came about such a trinket, but there're desperate folk who'd do you a harm for items of less value than this."

I noticed he dropped his voice as he said so and cast a wary eye on Wim, but this appeared unnecessary as the peddler paid us no mind at all.

Once I pinned the brooch into my waistband, as instructed, I became teary and Master Borlan tried to sooth me. "Now you mustn't cry," he said. "Master Wim doesn't want a wailing little girl on his hands all the way to Cros. Do you, Wim?"

"There's plague about. Don't touch me; don't breathe on me," was the peddler's only response.

"I won't cry," I promised Master Borlan and he nodded approvingly in a way that reminded me of Da.

"Can we be off now?" Wim demanded. "I've delayed long enough and the weather's not gettin' any better."

Master Borlan stepped down from the wagon and backed away. "Just you mind your word, Wim Erlin," he warned. "I'll hold you responsible if any harm befalls the child."

"Right, right," the peddler said impatiently. He snapped the reins and called to his horse, "Whitelegs, let's be off."

As the wagon started forward, I clung to the rattling seat. The peddler's old mare was faster than she looked and having never ridden in anything higher than our rickety farm cart, I was afraid of being thrown from my seat and run over beneath the tall wheels. By the time I screwed up the courage to lean over and peer around the side of the wagon, Master Borlan, standing beside the road, was already fading into the distance.

The wagon wheels splashed through pools of filthy water as we lurched down the rutted road. The driving rain had ended hours ago, but left its evidence in the deep mud and sodden leaves strewn across our path. The wind hadn't abated and I flinched each time I heard it stirring through the tree branches overhead, knowing another shower of cold droplets was about to be shaken loose to patter down on us. Occasionally, a ray of golden sunlight would peek from behind a thick layer of clouds and fall across our path, as if to taunt us with its promised warmth, but as suddenly as it appeared, it would be snatched away again, leaving us in this depressing world of gray.

The winding road we followed soon twisted and led us into a forest of firs and elder trees. Here, thick-trunked sentinels loomed over our path, hedging us in like rabbits in a snare, so that I had an uncomfortable desire to turn and head back out into the open. But if the peddler shared my unease, he kept it to himself as our wagon rolled steadily onward, until the grassy meadowland behind was lost from view.

The wood was still and heavy with shadows. Only small patches of overcast sky revealed themselves through the green canopy overhead and nothing stirred the foliage on either side of the road. There was a sameness to the passing scenery, and every towering tree, every splintered trunk or thick stand of ferns looked like the one before it.

I shivered, scarcely feeling my frozen fingers and toes, and wished Master Wim would stop and build a fire to warm us. But he never gave any indication he noticed the weather, and he appeared perfectly comfortable in his heavy cloak and sturdy boots. Perhaps he didn't feel the bite of the wind through the strips of wool twined about his hands.

I was surreptitious in my studying of the peddler because he made it plain early on that he wanted nothing to do with me. I wasn't to chatter or ask foolish questions such as when we would arrive at our destination or when we could eat. I had been ordered not to shift in my seat or to stand, as it would make the horse nervous.

Seeming all but oblivious to my presence now, the old man kept his gaze fixed on the road. He had one foot propped atop the wooden board at our feet and I noticed a crooked bend to that knee, which might have caused him to limp awkwardly when on foot. From time to time, he dropped a hand to massage the damaged joint and when he did, a grimace would spread across his features. They weren't particularly attractive features even without the scowl. His closely set eyes were a frosty shade of blue-grey, like ice over a winter pond, and his long nose bent sharply downward at the tip. His skin was like a faded map, with wrinkles for pathways and moles and age spots sprinkled around generously, like markers.

I was so intent on examining my companion's flaws that I noticed immediately when his brow furrowed in concern. Snapping my attention to the road ahead, I was met with an unexpected sight. We had just rounded a bend and we suddenly found ourselves facing an obstacle. A thick tree lay fallen on its side, covering the full width of our path and blocking any traffic that might have passed. The trunk was so wide a large man couldn't have reached both arms around its base, let alone have a hope of shifting it an inch to either side.

But the tree didn't hold my gaze long, for my attention was swiftly drawn to the collection of rough-looking men clustered around it. There were half a dozen of them, dressed mostly in ragged clothing of dappled brown or green. A few were outfitted in mismatching pieces of leather armor or chainmail and here and there, daggers or short swords were in evidence. The men lacking blades were armed with quarterstaffs or cudgels and many of them carried bows. They were a lean and ragged looking lot, and even at a distance, menace was clearly written across their hard faces. Small as I was, I had the sense to be afraid.

Wim cried, "Brigands!"

He slapped the mare with his reins, urging her to speed. The frightened animal charged ahead, and I clung tight to the edge of my seat as we shot forward. The road was rocky and pitted and the wagon lurched alarmingly from side to side, and as we drew nearer to the obstacle ahead, I didn't know which danger was greater, that we would plow full-speed into the felled tree or that our wagon might tip before we reached that point and both of us would be crushed beneath it. Cold fear dug its claws into my belly and I squeezed my eyes shut.

Wim must have realized the disaster we drove toward, for at the last possible instant, he hauled back on the reins. Even braced as I was, I was nearly thrown from the wagon as we jolted to a sudden halt. I had been desperately wedging my toes against the footboard while bracing my back against the seat behind me, but neither precaution prevented my being slung sideways. My head smacked loudly against the back of the seat and I couldn't help crying out. Beside me, Wim seemed to have been jarred by the stop as well.

"Don't think about turning that rickety cart around," an unfamiliar voice warned us. "We chose this spot for the narrowness of the path."

I gaped at the speaker, an immense mountain of a man with a mane of wild, half-braided red hair that flowed to his waist. He towered at least a foot taller than an ordinary man and, with hands massive enough for uprooting saplings, looked as impassive a barrier as the fallen tree he stood atop. The men flanking him appeared to be awaiting a signal from this giant, but instead of giving one, he leapt down and strode toward us.

Wim glanced back the way we'd come and tightened his grip on the reins, but the big stranger was right. There was no room for turning our wagon around and the peddler must have been reluctant to leap to the ground and dash for escape. A man of his age had little hope of outrunning anyone, even without his crooked knee.

The giant seemed to follow Wim's thinking, too. "A wise decision, old bones," he said. "You wouldn't get far before my friends shot you down. They're always eager for some live target practice, although I fear you would make poor sport with that twisted leg."

Coming to lean easily against the side of the wagon, he tapped Wim's bad knee for emphasis. His height was even more impressive at this proximity and I noticed now the series of long, ridged scars slashed at an angle across his face, lending a hard look to features that might otherwise have been cheerful.

Ignoring my perusal, the big man said to Wim, "Now then, old man. Suppose we come to an agreement that will mutually benefit both of us and speed you on your way."

"You speak of robbery," Wim snarled.

"Not at all. Think of it, instead, as a much needed donation to the favorite cause of our band's captain."

"And what noble cause would that be?"

"Why, that of feeding himself and his good followers, of course," said the giant. "I can see you're a compassionate man who would never deny a handful of hungry strangers the coin to purchase a decent meal."

"Would it do any good to refuse what you've already decided to take from me?" Wim asked, glaring darkly.

"That's the spirit, good fellow," said the giant.

"Now empty your pockets into this little bag and be quick. My companions and I are wet, weary, and not our usual, patient selves today."

He produced a worn sack, which he extended with a little flourish, but Wim ignored the offering.

"The Praetor has no use for thieves in his province," he warned the big stranger. "Steal from an honest peddler today if it pleases you. But I warn you, soon enough you'll all be hunted down and hung."

"I won't argue with you, old man. I've advised you to pay the toll. If you lack sufficient coin, we won't mind helping ourselves to the goods in your wagon. No need to make a fuss. No one will be hurt so long as you cooperate, and I feel sure you'll have the wisdom to do just that."

But Wim, no longer cowed, said, "You vermin will see no coin from me and you'll keep your filthy hands off my wagon. I'll report you to the Praetor when I reach Selbius and see the lot of you arrested. I see many of you already bear a thieves brand, so the second offense means death."

He smiled grimly, as if already witnessing the lot of them swinging from a gallows.

One of the listening outlaws, a wiry man with a cudgel, showed his teeth. "Maybe we're too desperate to care," he said. "Maybe we're hungry enough to eat skinny old peddlers before they go running to the Praetor."

Wim licked his lips as if realizing he may have spoken too vehemently and his hand disappeared inside his cloak.

The giant broke in with, "Enough talk. Let's see some coin."

"Never," said Wim.

The big man shrugged and stepped back, saying, "Very well then. I fear we won't part on kindly terms." He nodded to his companions. "Fellows, see what you can do to persuade this old fool to change his mind, without killing him. Murders only make the way patrol more vigilant."

He settled himself on a nearby tree stump, as if preparing to watch some form of entertainment, while his companions closed in. In a flash, a burly man with a beard and shaved head seized me roughly by the neck of my cloak and tried to remove me from his way. Instinctively, I sank my teeth into his arm and, as the brigand thrashed, attempting to shake me loose, I was dragged out of the wagon and hit the ground headfirst. The pain stunned me and a fuzzy blackness ringed the edge of my vision. Dizzily, I tried to summon the inner flame of magic I had touched so effortlessly once before, but I couldn't find it.

When the world stopped turning and the pain and darkness receded, I remembered Wim. One brigand had grabbed the old man and was attempting to drag him down from his perch on the wagon seat. The peddler struggled and I saw the glint of steel as he retrieved a short knife from inside his cloak. He was about to plunge it into his attacker when the other man stabbed him first.

I stared, horrified, as the old man's lifeless body fell forward, landing heavily near me. A pool of crimson blood quickly pooled around him.

If I was frozen with shock, no one else was. The red-haired giant swooped in and struck the face of the man who had done the killing, shouting at him about disobeying orders, while the other brigands ignored the arguing men and swarmed over the wagon, quickly emptying it of anything of value. Although I was distantly aware of these activities, my mind scarcely took them in. I couldn't tear my gaze away from Wim's wide eyes, staring unseeing toward the treetops.

Someone came to stand over me. He was speaking, but I didn't respond, and when he waved a hand before my face, I ignored that as well, keeping my gaze fixed on Wim. Had my Mama's eyes stared blankly like that when she was dead? Had Da's?

"What have you there, Brig?" asked the redheaded giant, joining the man beside me.

"I don't know," the first one said. "A vicious little cur, I think. Bites like one, at least." He knelt and, with surprisingly gentle hands, turned my face away from Wim's corpse, asking, "Where are you from, child? Do you live nearby?" I recognized him as the man with the shaved head, whom I had bitten.

When I held my tongue, he tried again. "Do you have a name? What's your father's name?"

Again I refused to answer and the bald man

frowned, saying to the giant, "I don't know about this one, Dradac. What are we to do with it?"

The giant shrugged. "I think *it* is female—a little girl, to be exact. As to what's to be done with her, I suggest we leave her right here. She's no concern of ours."

"But she's only a wee one, isn't she? What if she dies or comes to some hurt?"

The giant said, "Don't care if she does. Children are a cursed plague. But I imagine someone will pass this way and find her in a day or so. If you're concerned, put her up on the mare and send her back the way she came."

It's a long ride to the nearest village," the bald man pointed out. "Do you think she's big enough to stay on the horse and keep it to the road?"

"How should I know? I'm not the one with children. Maybe we could tie her onto the horse?" As he spoke, the giant stooped to examine me more closely and winced, evidently unimpressed with what he saw. "Ugly little critter, isn't she? If we do save her, I don't think any future sweethearts will be thanking us. What's she got on her mouth?"

"My blood. She took a chunk out of my hand earlier. Look at it."

"A revolting sight. Let's leave the little biter to fend for herself."

"I don't feel I can do that."

"Then she's your problem," the giant said. "The rest of us are moving out. But a word of advice. If you're considering doing anything stupid, like bringing her back to camp, think again. Rideon would have both our hides."

The bald man was silent a moment before apparently coming to the same conclusion. He rose and turned away, following the other brigands as they tramped off into the underbrush.

After they were gone, I stirred enough to wrap my arms around myself as shivers wracked my body, not all of them from the cold. Even with my head averted, I couldn't get the memory of Wim's corpse out of my mind. I had seen many deaths lately.

I became aware of the sound of something large crashing through the underbrush. The noise grew nearer and then the returning brigand broke out onto the road.

Scooping me up in strong arms, the bald man said, "Come along then, little dog. I've been thinking on it and I cannot abandon you here."

At last I found my tongue. "I'm not a dog; I'm a girl. Dogs don't talk."

"And girls don't bite."

He lifted me up onto his broad shoulders and we moved off after the others, leaving the road, horse and wagon, and dead peddler behind.

CHAPTER THREE

I MUST HAVE FALLEN ASLEEP WHILE the man carried me, for I remember nothing of the trek to the outlaw camp. Awaking sometime later, I found myself lying amid an itchy pile of leaves heaped over a hard stone floor. The sound of voices had stirred me from my sleep. Looking into the surrounding darkness, I could see no one. I had no idea where I was but felt too weary to be afraid. For the first time in what seemed like a long time, I was warm and dry and that was enough to content me.

Nearby, I could hear a continuous roaring sound like the rushing of water, but it was impossible to identify what direction it came from. The darkness was deep and the noise echoed loudly around me, bouncing off the surrounding walls. It was strangely lulling and I lay still, eyes closed once more, listening to that mighty roar and feeling the fogginess of sleep rising up to claim me again. I no longer remembered what had awakened me.

Then a second noise filtered through my consciousness—a nagging buzz, a faint murmur at the edge of my hearing. Drowsily, I tried to ignore it, but the sound was persistent and grew louder, soon resolving itself into the low cadence of approaching voices. Men's voices, frightening and unfamiliar. I squeezed my eyes shut tighter and burrowed down into the mold-scented leaves as they drew nearer. I began to distinguish snatches of their conversation.

"Your little hound is snug enough in her leafy bed. Wish I could say the same for myself, but I'll not sleep a wink, wondering what he'll do when he hears about her. And he will hear. The Hand knows everything that happens in this forest."

A second, deeper voice answered. "We've a reprieve until morning. Surely by then we'll figure the best way of explaining everything."

The gaps in the conversation grew fewer the nearer they came, until the voices were hovering directly over me. I kept as still as a mouse beneath the shadow of a hawk. I was very aware of the little bits of dry leaves that had worked their way into my clothing and were itching against my skin now, but I dared not twitch so much as a muscle to relieve my discomfort.

"Easy for you to say, Brig," the first voice argued. "You're not the one he'll blame. I had charge of you all, so it's me that'll be taken to account for what went wrong."

"I'll take the responsibility on myself," his companion rumbled. "Bringing the child here was my idea and I'll own up to it."

"I wouldn't want to be in your place when

you do. And don't forget there's the dead man to account for as well. The Hand orders us to lie low for a bit and what do we do? We go and kill an old peddler and steal a child, either of which could call the Praetor's attention down on us."

I dared open my eyes into narrow slits just wide enough to peer up at the two shadowy figures standing over me. I recognized the giant named Dradac and the bald, bearded outlaw he called Brig.

Brig said, "I doubt there'll be much fuss over an old man found dead in a forest lane. The Praetor has bigger things on his mind."

"I hope you're right. But I reckon there'll be time enough to deal with our problems in the morning, after we've had a bit of rest," Dradac said.

His footsteps rang hollowly as he moved away, calling out, "What about you? Aren't you sleeping tonight? Kinsley says you've got the midnight watch."

"Right. Think I'll stay here until then and keep an eye on the little one."

The retreating footsteps hesitated. "Brig, you know the child's not yours to keep, right? You understand she can't stay long in Dimmingwood? The Hand would never allow it. Your sons are gone and Netta with them. There's no bringing your family back or replacing them with this girl."

"What do you know of my family?" Brig asked sharply. "What have you heard? Do the others joke about my story around the campfire?"

Dradac sounded placating. "Of course not. I don't think most people even remember what happened. You know there's no place in the band for any man's past or future. The here and now keeps us busy enough."

Satisfied I was in no immediate danger, my eyelids were growing heavy. The men's voices droned on, but I ceased to listen to the words. Drowsiness stole over me again and I dismissed the strange men and the itchy leaves against my skin. My bed was warm and soft and I slipped easily into a deep slumber.

It seemed like only a short time before I was awakened by a rough shaking.

"Wake up, little dog. You want to sleep the morning away?" a voice asked.

Strong hands took me beneath the arms, lifting me to my feet. Bleary eyed and confused, I tried in vain to find something familiar in my surroundings. I stood in a nook at the back of an immense cave, a thick pile of leaves heaped at my feet.

The muscular, bearded man with the shaved head loomed over me again, and I remembered his name. Brig. Rather than feeling frightened, I was strangely comforted by his presence. I was being looked after. There was nothing to fear.

He took my small hand in his large, callused one and wordlessly led me through a maze of dark warrens, a network of tunnels formed in stone. Dimly glowing lanterns hung at irregular intervals along the walls, providing a faint flickering light that illumined our steps. I was glad of the firm hand gripping mine, because alone I would have felt lost and frightened in this place. But with the big man beside me, it was an adventure.

One of the areas we passed was filled with crates and wooden barrels. Canvas sacks lined the walls and out of the open mouths of these peeked potatoes and dried beans. Cooking pots and overturned copper tubs were stored here also, and a stack of split kindling was piled in one corner. From the walls hung an assortment of various tools I didn't recognize. A polished silver tray and bowl set, incongruous in these surroundings, rested atop one barrel. Bundles of colorful silk were leaned carelessly against a wall, and from a wide-mouthed sack shoved forgotten into a corner a collection of glittering jewelry spilled onto the floor. I had no opportunity to stare, for Brig quickly led me past this alcove and into a larger low-ceilinged cavern.

Here I glimpsed tattered blankets and bed stuffs heaped around the floor and a scattering of personal belongings set atop wooden boxes or hung from the walls. Images and symbols had been painstakingly etched into the stone of ceiling and walls. There was a snarling bear's head, a leaping deer, and various other woodland creatures. In the center of the wall, one particular carving stood out, taking precedence over the others, a large impression of a man's hand, colored in red. I would have looked at that longer, but Brig never slowed, tugging me along at his side, and we left this area behind us.

The rushing, roaring sound I had been vaguely aware of since waking became louder now. We passed a small opening, through which a faint glow of daylight penetrated, and I had a brief glimpse of a foaming waterfall sheeting down over this window to the outside. Brig allowed me no opportunity to gape and the waterfall slipped out of my sight as quickly as it had appeared, its roar fading as we distanced ourselves from it.

Ahead, I caught sight of another small pinpoint of daylight. This grew larger as we approached, until it proved to be a man-sized hole, through which I could see trees and greenery. Brig pushed me out this exit ahead of him, and I stepped into the soft glow of early morning.

I stood in a large clearing, ringed on two sides by pines and giant elder trees and backed by the great formation of red rock behind me. A deep, clear stream ran along one side of the clearing, fed by the waterfall tumbling from the rocks over the cave. A fire pit marked the center of the camp, and a number of men sat around the flames, resting on overturned logs or on bare earth. There were about a dozen outlaws in the camp, some of them eating or busying themselves with chores, others sitting back at their ease. One carried an armload of fresh kindling. A pair of others tended the campfire and the kettle bubbling over it.

The scent emanating from that stewpot made

my stomach rumble, but my companion dragged me past it. I was led straight across the clearing and into the shadow of the trees. Here a man wearing nothing but his breeches sat on an overturned keg. His back was toward us and he leaned forward to study his reflection on the surface of a polished copper plate that had been nailed onto the tree before him. At our approach, he didn't pause from the task of scraping stubble from his chin with a sharpened blade.

I studied the back of his head with less interest than I would have felt for a taste of whatever had been cooking in that stewpot. His black hair was cropped so close you could see the shape of his skull. His arms and back were well muscled, but I thought, if standing, he would probably be the shortest man present. I found him less impressive than the red-haired giant, Dradac, or even Brig at my side.

"So. This is the source of all the trouble, is it?" the stranger asked, finally turning to look me over.

I was startled by the intensity of his deeply set jewel-green eyes, which stood out starkly against tanned skin. Such bright eyes were rare in magickless people. His face was long and narrow, his cheekbones prominent above a sharply crooked nose that looked as if it had been broken many times. Several small scars decorated his face and a number of larger ones were visible across his chest.

Even newly awakened to my magic as I was, I sensed there was something dangerous about this man, that he had the power to make people think and do as he chose. Under his penetrating gaze, I forsook my attempt to stare him down and ducked behind Brig's leg to hide. It was a reaction so natural in the face of this stranger and his cold eyes that I was scarcely even aware of doing it.

The motion did not escape notice. The jewel-eyed man laughed—a harsh barking sound that held no warmth. "You see that, men?" He raised his voice to the nearest outlaws. "The runt is frightened of me. Am I such a terrible sight, then? Brig, a fine pet you've taken in. I've seen dead fish with more backbone." Then, "Look me in the eye, child!" he demanded sternly of me. "Do you know who I am?"

I stared at him, silent.

He seemed not to mind. If anything, I thought he enjoyed my nervousness as he said, "I am the outlaw leader they call Rideon the Red Hand. Or simply *the Hand* to my more intimate friends and enemies. And how did I come by that name, you must be asking yourself?"

He leaned in close, as if about to impart a secret, and answered his own question. "I'll tell you how. I earned it by hard deeds and rebellion against the Praetor's laws. Look here at these hands, child."

I stared at the hands he extended palms upward and saw nothing remarkable. They were dirty, work-roughened hands with short, uneven nails.

"There's blood on them!" he barked suddenly so that I flinched.

I didn't see any blood but thought it might make him angry if I said so. He leaned back and regarded me as if disappointed by my lack of reaction. I had no notion what he expected of me and we simply stared at one another until he seemed to tire of it, asking abruptly, "What name does your family call you by, girl?"

I was too uneasy to speak, but an observer behind us put in with a laugh, "Brig calls her Little Dog."

We had become the center of attention in the camp and the other outlaws stopped their tasks to observe our encounter. The outlaw named Rideon appeared to enjoy having an audience.

"Dog, eh? I think I would call her a little rabbit. She has all the pluck of one."

A round of amused laughter followed this statement and when it died, Rideon addressed Brig. "And what exactly do you plan on doing with this child? I'm given to understand it was your notion to bring her here."

There was no mistaking the displeasure in his voice.

Brig was prepared for the question. "She can't stay among us; I understand that well enough. I figure I'll search around for any family to claim her. If I can't find any living, I'll leave her in one of the woods villages, where folk will surely see that she's not allowed to starve."

Rideon said flatly, "I've a more practical solution. Drown her."

Brig didn't seem to know what to make of that. "You're jesting," he said, but he sounded uncertain.

"Not at all. It'd be simple enough. We've a convenient stream on hand. No, wait... We wouldn't want to foul the drinking water, would we? Better yet, break her neck and bury her someplace away from camp."

Brig sounded dismayed. "I could never do that. Not to a little one."

A threatening note crept into Rideon's voice. "Are you refusing to obey your captain's orders?"

The surrounding outlaws moved back a little, bloodthirsty anticipation in their eyes.

Brig appeared to choose his words carefully. "No," he responded at length. "Not refusing, just asking for a reason. Why should she die? What harm is she to anyone?"

At his mild response, the tension in the air subsided and Rideon leaned back to study the bald man thoughtfully. "Very well," he said. "I'm a reasonable man and I've no objection to answering an honest question. The truth is, you've only yourself to thank for the girl's fate. She must die because she's seen too much—things we can't afford to have become common knowledge. I shouldn't have to explain the obvious to you. Just imagine, wouldn't the Fists love to know where we're hiding?"

"But she's so small," Brig argued. "She slept in my arms most of the journey and could never find her way here again, let alone lead others. Who would listen to such a child anyway?"

Rideon considered me. There was no dislike in his eyes. To either like or dislike me wasn't worth his effort, any more than he would have troubled himself to bear ill will toward an ant. "You're certain she couldn't return, leading our enemies along behind her?" he asked. "Certain enough to risk all our lives on it?"

"I'm sure of it," Brig said.

I stood by quietly, listening to this exchange but not feeling terribly afraid for my life. I instinctively trusted Brig to protect me. It hardly occurred to me to wonder if or why he would.

Brig continued. "It's not a far walk to Coldstream, and if I travel all night after dropping her there, I can be back at camp by morning."

"And leave others to do your duties and take over your watch for you, I suppose?"

Brig had no answer planned for that, but one of his comrades saved him by speaking up. "I'll stand in for him," the outlaw said. "It's only for a day anyway. We done rescued the runt from starving on the road. It's only fitting we see her through to safety."

There arose a noise of general agreement at these words.

Rideon looked around him and must have seen the novelty of a generous deed appealed to his followers. The dangerous spark fled from his eyes and he appeared reconciled to the idea.

"Of course it is fitting. We will do right by the

child," he said, as though the plan had been his own, and he told Brig to make preparations for our journey straight away.

Now that my fate was decided, I lost interest in the big peoples' conversation. The other spectators also appeared to grow bored as they realized there would be no physical confrontation between Brig and their captain, and they drifted away.

My belly loudly proclaimed its emptiness and, propelled by my hunger, I wandered from Brig's side and over to the campfire. The redheaded giant, Dradac, and some others were seated on stumps before the flames. Dradac was occupied with fletching a stack of shaved wooden shafts at his feet. He whistled a cheerful tune as he worked and, observing my longing looks toward the stewpot, soon took pity on me.

"Hungry, little dog?" he asked.

When I nodded eagerly, he spooned up a portion of warm venison stew into a carved wooden bowl.

"Don't feed the hound, Dradac. It'll think it can hang around the table," another outlaw joked as I fell to.

But the giant only laughed and refilled my bowl each time it came up empty, until I could hold no more. I was just setting my bowl aside when Brig appeared out of nowhere to collect me, and we left the camp, setting off on a long trek through the forest.

Here my clearest memories of that time come to an end. I recall nothing of the journey to the woods village of Coldstream, nor of Brig setting me down near its sheltering walls and shooing me in the proper direction. All I know is the tale I grew up hearing from the outlaws of how Brig made the return journey alone that night and of how, within two days time, I showed up at their camp again. Everyone said I must have put my nose to the ground like a true hound and traced Brig's tracks.

Further attempts were made to pry me from my chosen home. But I clung to the leg of Brig, whom I had claimed as mine, and resisted relocation so loudly and vehemently the brigands were moved by my determination—or perhaps merely exhausted by it. "It's a ferocious little hound you've got there, Brig," one outlaw remarked admiringly.

Eventually, Rideon was called in to make his wishes known. I remember huddling against Brig, shivering and half-frozen after my return trek from the woods village. I stared up at the outlaw leader and Rideon the Red Hand gazed down on me coldly.

He spared us a long suspense, declaring emotionlessly, "The hound may stay. From this day on, she will live and work among us and be treated as one of ours. And, as she cannot remain a hound forever, today I also give her a name. Ilan, after a faithful tracker I once had. That stenched dog could trail a mole through a snowstorm."

"What changed your mind about the girl?" Brig asked. "Why is she to stay?"

Rideon glared. "Because if we attempt to remove

her, she'll only continue returning to us, thanks to your refusal to dispose of her. Also, because morale is low and the child's spirit appeals to the men. But most of all, because I order it."

After this there could be no further discussion of the matter. I stayed. Although the decision came from Rideon, the other outlaws appeared generally in agreement that I was to be Brig's responsibility. After all, it was to him I'd attached myself, so it was only natural he should have the care of me.

During this space of time, all that had previously occurred in my life swiftly came to seem like a distant memory and, plunging into a new world, I lost sight of anything connected with the old.

CHAPTER FOUR

MEMORIES OF MY EARLY DAYS among the band of forest brigands are hazy. Seasons changed, the weather warmed to summer, and then winter stole over the land again. My first winter in Dimmingwood was a hard one. Food was scarce that year and I was not yet accustomed to living outdoors in such weather. Brig worried aloud over how skinny I grew and seemed to think I would die when I succumbed to my first winter chill. But soon, winter's icy grip was lifted from the province and spring found me alive and thriving.

I set into my new existence with enthusiasm. I loved the woods and the forest creatures, loved the scent of pine and the rustle of the wind in the treetops. This world of leaf and shadow, bramble and stream, quickly became mine. There were no other children here and only one or two women came and went around the camp, but I never felt lonely.

Brig was my closest companion and I followed at his heels sunup to sundown, drinking in all I saw. I learned early to tell one tree from another, until I knew my way around the wood better than many of the grown men. Soon, Brig was training me to track and hunt small game.

My skill in another area was expanding as well. Now that my magical talent had prematurely awakened, it refused to fall dormant again and made itself known in a series of unpleasant ways. My sickness that first winter was more than an ordinary chill. I was alternately hot and cold, shivering and feverish. Too weak to stand, I lay miserably on a deerskin pallet in the shelter of the cave for weeks. Weight dropped off me until I was little more than a wraith, and evil dreams plagued me in the night. Not dreams of home or of my mother, but twisted, confused nightmares I could scarcely recall upon waking. I always awoke trembling, with a premonition of doom hanging over me, as if the dreams foreshadowed terrible events to come. Occasionally, I visited a strange place while I slept, a world of paths and mists, but when I woke, I could never remember much of what I saw there.

By the end of the first winter month, I began to improve, to Brig's obvious relief. But I didn't emerge from the illness unchanged. I regained my strength and my weight, but a strange new effect came about. One moment I would be stirring a pot of stew at the fire. The next, I would become abruptly aware that Brig was angry and fighting with someone, though it was happening at such a distance I couldn't possibly see or hear anything of the disagreement. I simply felt his anger. Other times, I might be sleeping and would wake suddenly, startled by the sense of a pair of men approaching camp from the south. It usually proved to be just two of our members returning from a long hunt, but it was disturbing that I should know of their coming before they were near enough for our sentries to spot them.

If my mother or anyone else with the magic had been present, I could have spoken to them of this. But as it was, I was surrounded by magickless and there was no one to guide me. I had come into my magic early and, doubtless, my parents had thought they had plenty of time ahead to prepare me for this. There was only one person I could go to now.

When I revealed what I was going through to Brig, he seemed disturbed. Frightened even. He knew no way to help me with this problem—and a problem it obviously was in his mind.

"But I'll take care of you, Ilan," he assured me, "and between the two of us we'll find our way through this."

He made me swear I would never speak of my magical abilities to anyone else and suggested I cease using them. I told him that was impossible. The magic had come to me and though I might have given it up to please Brig if it were in my power, something told me *it* would never give *me* up.

I didn't understand Brig's fear of magic. I had little knowledge of the cleansings happening throughout the province and rarely remembered the strange words of the Fist who had chased me into the woods on the night of my parents' deaths. For now, I knew only that Brig appeared anxious and disappointed with me.

Over time, I grew accustomed to my new abilities and developed a limited understanding of what I could and couldn't do with them. My main talent was sensing other presences around me. At odd moments I was also granted flickering glimpses of people's emotions, which often helped me guess at their plan or intent before it became clear to others.

In those days I spent nearly every waking moment in the company of the bald, bearded outlaw and he, as if sensing my need for the stability he offered, didn't begrudge me his time. If for any reason he was unavailable, Dradac would step into his place as my caretaker.

I was growing and quickly learning to care for myself. As the youngest member of the outlaw band, I often fell into the role of camp drudge, but I considered hauling water, scrubbing crockery, and running messages a small price to pay for the excitement and adventure of living among the brigands. I was a pet to a handful of the men like Brig, who had once had children or younger siblings. Even the sterner outlaws were won over by my admiration and fascination with everything they did. They regaled me with exaggerated tales, saved choice bits of food for me, and would bring me little trinkets when they returned from their forays.

And so time ran on, the days so full from dawn to dusk that the passing years felt like moments. I could no longer recall vividly the faces of my parents, except in the rare nightmare, and on the occasions when I thought of the little farm where I'd once lived, my memories were hazy, less real than any dream.

I still possessed my mother's brooch. Brig had found it on me at some time or other and had thoughtfully stored it away until I was old enough to have it. The circumstances surrounding that trinket were still confused in my mind, but I always regarded it with a touch of reverence. It was a treasure from a past I only dimly recalled, to be pulled out occasionally and wondered at, then tucked safely away again. Once, I had examined it closely enough to find it had tiny writing engraved across the back. But I could neither write nor read and knew no one who could, so the meaning of the letters on the brooch remained a mystery.

My thirteenth winter saw my body changing. I was taller now and my tunics grew tight over my breasts, which had begun to swell alarmingly. I knew this was natural at my age but was uncomfortable with the change and longed for everything to go back to the way it had been last year. Occasionally, I would steal peeks at myself in the now battered copper platter Rideon still used as a shaving mirror, but these glimpses always ended in disappointment. I don't know what I hoped to see, but what I found was a plain, skinny girl, whose legs looked too long for her body. My pale face was narrow, my nose too long and sharp for beauty. My pointed ears stuck out unattractively from my head. But at least no one ever commented on the silvery hair or pale skin I had inherited from my mother's people. Skeltai ancestry was common this close to the Provincial border and wasn't necessarily accompanied by the gift of magic. Besides, our band already had a giant in our midst and a man who was rumored to be half-goblin, so I fit into the menagerie surprisingly well.

That winter stretched long and bitter and when it released the land from its icy grip and the warmth of spring stole into the air, our camp reawakened in a fresh bustle of activity. Travelers and merchant caravans were on the move again and the brigands were eager to plunder the goods and coin they had seen little of during the frozen season.

Our band had swollen in size and there were now several dozen of us divided over two camps, Red Rock cave and Molehill. Our numbers shifted constantly as Rideon was forever sending groups on forays to the edges of Dimmingwood. Occasionally they didn't return, but there were always more to fill their places. The band of Rideon the Red Hand had established a name and we had a constant flow of thieves eager to join our ranks.

I asked Dradac one day, "Why do people flock to Rideon? He certainly bears no affection for them.

He would allow any of us to die without hesitation if it were profitable for him."

Dradac didn't look up from the chunk of wood he whittled. "Deep thoughts for such a sunny day, little hound," he answered. "In my experience, outlaws are less interested in being valued than in being led well. Rideon's sharp wits are all that stand between us and the hangman's noose, and the rest of the band know it. Besides, even thieves and killers like a hero, and it takes something powerful to inspire us in these plague-cursed times."

"Plague's long over," I murmured absently.

"Aye, I know that. But its shadow hangs on. You can see it in the eyes of the man who lost all his sons in that single plague year, and it left its mark in the new graves spread across the province. I still smell the fear on the wind, mingled with the smoke from the fires…"

His voice trailed off, but I knew what he was thinking. The occasional accused sorcerer was still found once in awhile and put to the penalty of the law. They burned them these days. No one was going to risk another plague. I didn't know what Dradac's views on magic were and I wasn't about to ask him, but I was ever mindful of Brig's advice to keep my ability to myself.

I looked out over the spreading treetops below. Perched high in the thick boughs of a tree a few miles beyond the perimeter of Red Rock, we were on morning watch. Or rather, Dradac was on watch and I sat with him, pretending the task was mine too.

When a shrill birdcall split the air I was so lost in my thoughts that I started and nearly fell from my precarious perch. The bad imitation of a crested redbird was a familiar signal, one that meant trespassers were approaching the perimeters of the camp.

Dradac winced. "That's Seirdric. I'd know that strangled warble anywhere. Come on."

"What do you think it is?" I demanded, scrambling down the tree after him and following as he slipped into the underbrush.

"Probably only innocent travelers blundering through the forest. Looks like you'll have an opportunity to see a bit of action today."

I kept my thoughts to myself, reluctant to remind him Brig preferred to keep me far away from "action." Torn between eagerness and unease at witnessing whatever was to come, my nerves fluttered skittishly. But excitement won out. I had waited a long time to be considered old enough for this sort of thing. I wondered if Dradac would kill anyone. Then I wondered if *I* might kill anyone. I had a sturdy staff with me just in case.

Following our man's call, Dradac moved swiftly and silently through the forest so that I had difficulty keeping pace with him. It was easy to locate our quarry as we drew near. They made a great deal of noise, crashing clumsily through the underbrush and conversing in loud, angry tones. We heard them long before we caught sight of them.

"You had better know what you're about, you impudent scoundrel. I've paid dear coin for safe escort to the abbey and if I find you've gone and lost us in this gloomy wood—"

"You'll stutter, puff up your fat jowls, and do nothing at all. You cannot frighten me, priest, so save your breath and your threats for someone else."

"Why y-you mother-forsaken black heart! How d-d-dare you?" In his indignation, the priest was so overcome by his impediment he had difficulty spitting out the words.

His companion ignored his complaint. "I've told you before, Honored One, you've nothing to fear. I know this wood like the back of my hand. It's but a shorter path I lead you on."

"I should have been content to r-remain on the road," the priest replied sullenly. "But now that it's too late to turn back, at least lead us on with a little more speed. I'd as soon be out of this forest by nightfall. They say these woods are crawling with murderous brigands."

He paused to call over his shoulder to a third companion. "You, boy! Have a care with my belongings. That's not a sack of potatoes you're carrying."

Dradac and I crept closer until we had a full view of the trespassers. There were three of them. A large, balding fellow led the way, followed by a chubby, elderly man dressed in the traditional gray robes of an Honored One, a priest of the Light.

Trailing these two was a slender boy of about my age, also wearing priestly robes and carrying a heavy pack across his shoulders.

The path they followed would soon lead the travelers straight past us. Dradac and I had dropped to our bellies, concealing ourselves in a tall patch of waving toadsbreath. A glance at the trees to our right revealed two of our men, Illsman and Nib, concealed in the branches of a pair of thick elder trees. To our left, the swaying of a low stand of shrubbery gave away Seirdric's position.

Imitating Dradac, I kept my head low as we crouched in the greenery, and as we waited for the approaching strangers, I used the time to size up the three unlikely traveling companions. The lead man had the appearance of a woodsman by his deer-hide boots, the wolf skin thrown over his tunic, and the long hunting knife at his belt. He was older, balding, and his wide belly was more gut than muscle.

I moved my attention to the elderly priest. Despite his age, the Honored One was neither thin nor frail, but bore a round, fleshy frame. Trotting along in the woodsman's wake, he puffed continually, his round cheeks pink with the exertion of moving his bulk to keep stride. Occasionally, he turned and snapped an order at the skinny boy trailing him and the unfortunate boy would labor to pick up his pace.

The youth was of slim build with little muscle and it was obvious the burden he carried was too great for his size. But his wide jaw was set in an appearance of determination and despite his obvious weariness, there was a gleam of excitement in his eyes, as if he were so eager to reach his destination he didn't care what conditions he was forced to endure along the way. He chewed his lower lip as he stumbled on, all but tripping over the hem of his ill-fitting robes. His dark hair was worn in a similar fashion to that of the old Honored, cropped so closely his pale scalp showed. His eyes, squinted against the beads of sweat trailing from his forehead, caught my attention. They were widely spaced and an odd, deep-violet hue.

The three strangers were passing just in front of us when Dradac suddenly revealed our presence. Rising from our hiding place, he called, "Hold, friends. We mean you no harm."

The woodsman in the lead whipped around, startled. His eyes widened at the sight of us and his hands immediately came up to fumble for something over his shoulder.

Dradac must have noticed the motion, for he called, "You have nothing to fear from us, so long as you draw no—"

He was cut off abruptly, for the woodsman had found what he sought. In a sudden motion, he pulled free the weapon, raising and loosing it before anyone could react. Instinctively, I ducked, but I was not his target. I saw Dradac's body jerk awkwardly and then he swayed sharply to one side, a stunned expression on his face. A red stain bloomed across his tunic, where a crossbow bolt lodged deeply into his left shoulder. I stared in horror from the giant to the small crossbow the stranger now held leveled at me.

CHAPTER FIVE

I COULDN'T HAVE MOVED JUST THEN even had I known what action to take. Fortunately, I didn't have to. With enraged shouts, the other outlaws leapt from their hiding places and felled the woodsman before he could prepare another bolt. My view was momentarily blocked as they wrestled him to the ground. There followed a short frenzy of motion, a series of strangled screams, and when next I got a look at our enemy, he lay still upon his back. I stared stupidly at the blood-soaked tunic clinging wetly to his chest. Our own men had as much blood spattered on their clothes and hands, but none appeared to be theirs.

"There's one will never trouble us again," Illsman said, grimly swiping a speck of blood off his chin.

I couldn't tear my eyes from the lifeless corpse lying in the grass at the outlaw's feet. The world seemed to be spinning around me. I was vaguely aware of frantic muttering sounds in the background—the terrified priest chanting a desperate prayer. I couldn't focus on his words, but dropped to my knees and doubled over. My stomach heaved and then I was vomiting my breakfast onto the ground and all over my boots. I wretched until my belly was empty, then as I drew in one deep breath after another, the dizziness subsided and I became aware again of the world around me.

I saw that Dradac had collapsed to his knees, face drained pale and forehead resting against a tree. Nearby, Illsman was stripping the woodsman's corpse of weapons and anything of value. Meanwhile, Seirdric and Nib were advancing, blades drawn, on the two remaining strangers. The plump priest stood immobile, eyes squinted tightly closed and face turned heavenward, his lips moving in silent prayer. He made no move to flee or to defend himself as the brigands closed in. The same could not be said of his young companion.

"Run, Honored One. I'll defend you!" the boy cried, leaping boldly forward to shield his master. With determined force, he struck out with the only weapon he had, his travelers pack. Nib was caught unprepared as the heavy pack slammed into him and knocked him from his feet. Seirdric was not so easily felled. Before the boy could gather his strength, the outlaw slashed a knife down the lad's skinny ribs.

Yowling in pain, the boy dropped his pack and collapsed heavily to the ground. There, he curled into a tight ball, clutching his wounded side. A steady stream of blood appeared from beneath his hands. Behind him, the priest found the courage to turn and flee toward the near trees. Illsman snatched up the dead woodsman's crossbow and steadied it against his shoulder, aiming at the priest's retreating back, but no bolt was ever loosed.

"Stop!" Dradac shouted. "Let him go."

Illsman hesitated and during that pause, missed his opportunity. The priest had put the trees between them and was lost from sight.

"Why did you stop me?" Illsman growled. "I had a clean shot. Now we'll have to chase him down."

Dradac clutched his shoulder and spoke through gritted teeth. "Forget the old man—it's unlucky to murder a priest. Besides, he doesn't know the forest. He'll stumble around in circles for days before he finds his way free of the trees, and once his safety is secured, I very much doubt he'll have the courage to return."

A low moan nearby distracted me from the outlaws' conversation. I followed the sound to the priest boy, who writhed in pain a few yards from me. I don't know what instinct or pity made me move toward him, but I did. He lay on his side, hands fumbling uselessly at his injury. To his credit, he wasn't crying out. Instead, he sucked in his breath in ragged gasps against the pain. His hands were trembling, his knuckles white where he clenched handfuls of his gray robe in his fists, vainly attempting to slow the flow of blood.

His feeble efforts moved me and, unthinkingly, I began to assist him. Trying to remember what little I had learned from our camp healer about tending such injuries, I tore the hem of the boy's robe, ripping free a long strip of coarse cloth. With effort, I lifted him a few inches from the ground and shifted him enough to twine the bandage twice around his waist, pulling it tight over his injured side to staunch the bleeding. He gasped at the movement and the painful pressure against the wound, but I ignored his reaction, feeling a small surge of satisfaction when I saw the blood flowing less freely. The boy's face was growing pale as milk.

He opened violet eyes to peer into my face, and I was immediately struck by his gaze. It held none of the panicked dread I'd expected. Slowly, cautiously, I opened my magical sense to the turmoil of his emotions, only to discover there *was* no turmoil. Intrigued, I dug deeper but could find no fear in him, only a silent cry of determination and a strong will to live. Alongside this, hot waves of agony rippled through him, and I instinctively withdrew before the pain could reach through him and touch me.

I became aware once more of my companions. Dradac, his voice taut with pain, was giving orders. "Seirdric, stay behind and dispose of the bodies. I don't want anybody stumbling over this mess and wondering how it got here. Nib, you'll help him and Illsman will accompany me back to camp. I don't know that I can make it there on my own."

There were murmurs of agreement as the men leapt to obey his orders. And then they noticed me kneeling over the boy.

"What have you done here, hound?" Seirdric came over to frown down on me. "The boy should've bled to death. Now I'll have to finish him."

"No, leave him be," I said, not stopping to consider where I found the courage to speak so firmly. "He's no older than me. Let's give him a chance."

"Sure, a chance to stab us all in the backs," Seirdric snorted, drawing his knife.

Unthinkingly, I moved to shield the boy from his reach, but the big man shoved me aside easily.

Desperate for support, I cried, "Dradac, help me!"

"What is it, Ilan?" the giant asked impatiently. On his feet and leaning weakly on Illsman's shoulder, his face was sleeked with sweat at the effort it cost him to stand.

I felt genuine concern for him but had to trouble him anyway. "The priest boy still lives," I said. "Let me try and help him."

The giant looked beyond me to the boy's crumpled form. "Wake up, hound," he said. "That one's beyond saving even were we of a mind to. Come now and lend me your arm before I collapse."

But I wouldn't be swayed. "Just let me try," I begged. "I know I can save him." I actually knew nothing of the sort, but I wouldn't admit to doubts.

To my surprise, Dradac gave in, ordering Nib to carry the boy. He added, "I doubt he'll last out the day, but if he's another priest... Well, I won't have his blood on my hands. We'll let him die in a more comfortable bed at least, if the trip doesn't kill him."

The rest of the day was difficult. Between the two of us, Illsman and I were able to get Dradac back to camp with Nib trailing behind, carrying the unconscious priest boy. At first, Dradac leaned heavily on Illsman and I for support, but eventually his legs could no longer hold him. He was too heavy for Illsman to carry alone and so I was sent ahead to fetch what help I could. Eventually, with a strong man at either end of him, we were able to drag the giant in. After that point I lost track of what befell him, for I had to worry about the priest boy.

I chose an out of the way spot at the clearing's edge, near the stream draining from the pool below the fall. I would have liked to put the injured boy under some sort of shelter, but the cave would be too dim and I knew I'd need good lighting. After Nib deposited the lad on the hard ground, I persuaded him to stand by while I cut a pile of pine boughs for him to roll the boy onto. After that, the outlaw disappeared, leaving me alone to care for my charge and to wonder what I had got myself into.

I was glad to see the boy's bleeding had stemmed, but nervousness tinged my relief. I fiercely wanted him to live, even as I wondered at the strength of my determination. Yet now I was left with the question of what to do for him next. I sought out Javen, the camp healer. Healing was perhaps too optimistic a word for what Javen did, but he was a cobbler in his old life and was accustomed to stitching up the outlaws after their brawls or when someone took a blade. If any of us were ill, it was Javen who prepared the bitter draughts that occasionally helped but more often didn't.

I hadn't far to look. I found him examining Dradac, who was laid out near the mouth of the cave. But when I explained my need, Javen only responded distractedly with, "We've our own to see to just now, hound." The most I could extract from him was a promise to look in on the boy after he finished removing the bolt from Dradac's shoulder. I doubted a healer's presence would be needed by then, for it was unlikely the boy could survive that long.

Frustrated, I returned to my charge. I guessed he must have awakened temporarily during my absence because he had obviously been thrashing around. He was unconscious again now, but his weak efforts had loosened his crude bandage and fresh blood was visible, soaking through the cloth. I realized with dismay that I could rewrap him, but each time he moved, he would begin bleeding all over again.

As I looked on, he stirred in his sleep, gave a pained whimper, and was still again. Even as he slept, his pale, sweat-streaked face was drawn into a grimace of pain. I felt a wave of pity for him because he looked so young and helpless and, clenching my jaw, I went to work with renewed determination. I wouldn't think of failure.

The noises I heard in the background told me they were removing the bolt from Dradac's shoulder now, but, concentrating on my own task, I tried not to hear the giant's cries. I removed the boy's gray robes and clumsily worked him out of the tunic he wore beneath them. Then I bellowed for Nib, and incredibly, the outlaw answered my summons. With an authority that surprised even me, I ordered him to heat a kettle of water and fetch me anything that might serve as clean bandaging. He moved quickly to obey and I didn't stop to wonder why he followed my bidding. My mind was taken up with the task at hand.

I wadded the boy's dirty robe and applied it with pressure to the gash in his side, attempting to hold back the blood. I longed for Brig to appear just then and take this responsibility off my hands, but he didn't materialize and I knew he wouldn't. He was visiting the camp at Molehill and the vagueness I felt when reaching for him told me what a long distance separated us.

Nib returned with the objects I required and surprised me by crouching nearby to await further commands. I was glad of his company. His presence wouldn't allow me to display fear or doubt. When I peeled the blood-soaked bandage back from the boy's wound, a crimson stream trickled out, and I despaired. How could I clean the wound when it wouldn't stop bleeding? Reapplying the cloth, I rubbed the sweat from my brow with one arm, buying myself a little time.

Nib suggested helpfully, "Don't know much about these things, but it seems to me you should wait for the blood to clot before you take the bandage away."

"I know that," I lied, as I looked down on the boy I was struggling to save and asked myself why I was doing this for a complete stranger. I didn't even know his name.

The minutes ticked by. I expected the boy would slip away at any moment but his breathing held steady. His bleeding had miraculously ceased by the time Javen appeared—I had little idea how. At the healer's request, I stayed nearby over the next hour, watching as he bathed and stitched the priest boy's wound and applied fresh bandaging. Javen warned me it was unlikely my charge would survive the night.

At length, the healer departed, declaring he had done all he could. As soon as he had gone, I began constructing a shelter of sorts around the boy. It hardly felt right to let him lay out in the cold all night. Dusk was falling as I tramped into the forest to collect a heap of pine boughs and elder branches. I propped these limbs against one another and bound them with bits of twine, as Brig taught me, to form a flimsy shelter over the ground. More than likely it would blow over with the first gust of wind, I thought, standing back to eye the completed work.

About then I became aware of a savory scent

wafting on the evening breeze. One of the men had killed a wild boar and was now roasting it over the campfire. The sight and smell of the food set my empty stomach rumbling and, with a backward glance, I left my little shelter and went to the fire where for a short time I forgot my worries over a greasy slab of meat.

After eating, I remembered Dradac. Abandoning my place at the fire, I ducked into the cave, but on entering, found the giant sleeping deeply, laid out on a thick pallet of animal skins. His face was relaxed and I was relieved to see he wasn't in pain at the moment. I decided not to wake him and slipped silently back out into the gathering darkness.

I fetched bread and water for the priest boy, but found when I peered into his shelter that he still slept. A mercy, I supposed, as I sank to the earth to eat the dried bread myself. On finishing, I was assailed by a great weariness. The day's events had been more than I was accustomed to. The camp was silent around me, the other men having departed either to their beds or to their watches. I thought of turning to my own bed, but it seemed wrong to crawl into a warm, safe place while the injured boy slept out here. I moved my sleeping pallet out of the cave and into the shelter, piling my blankets and animal skins over the boy.

Just enough space remained for me to crawl inside and curl up on the hard ground beside him. Rocks jutted into my flesh and insects crawled over me, but I was accustomed to such discomforts.

Harder to ignore was the chill that descended as the ground cooled. I shivered and wrapped my arms around myself, eventually slipping into a shallow, miserable sleep.

I was awakened sometime during the night by the commotion of the priest boy groaning and tossing around. A thrashing elbow caught me in the face. I shoved aside the last remnants of sleep clouding my brain and reached out for him. Although he stilled at my touch, his rapid panting never slowed.

"Hurts..." He gritted out weakly.

"I know," I said. "But you need to relax. Squirming will only make it worse."

His response was so faint I had to lean closer to hear. "Am I going to die?" he gasped.

Admitting I didn't know would hardly soothe his fears. He was going to need all the courage he could summon over the next days. "You're going to be fine," I assured him. "It's a minor wound, not as bad as it feels."

"How bad?" he persisted. "Can I see it?"

"Maybe later. It's too dark in here now."

"Where's here?"

"Dimmingwood," I said. "You were journeying through the forest with a priest and an escort, remember? You were attacked by brigands, injured, and brought back to the outlaw camp. I'm Ilan and I'm looking after you."

He groaned. "I remember now. But where is Thilstain?"

"Would that be the balding woodsman with the belly?" I questioned.

"No, Honored Thilstain is a priest. The other was just a stranger, hired to safeguard us on the way to Whitestone Abbey."

"I'm afraid your escort is dead," I told him. "I don't know what became of the old priest. The last I saw of him was his back as he fled into the trees."

The boy sighed, sounding relieved. "So he has escaped? Then he may return with aid."

"I doubt that," I said. "He doesn't know where you are or even if you're alive. Besides, I imagine he's too giddy with joy just now over his own safety to spare much thought for yours."

I sensed the boy's disappointment, but all he said was, "Even if he can't help me, I suppose the fact that he escaped is cause for thankfulness. I wouldn't wish him harm, dour man though he was. No, I shouldn't have said that. It's wrong to criticize a man of the robe. Please, forget you heard it."

I grinned into the darkness. "I'm scarcely in a position to think less of you for a stray comment. An outlaw has greater wrongs to her credit."

He sounded suddenly alert. "You're one of those murderous thieves, then?"

"I'm afraid so," I said dryly. "But you've no cause to fear me. Even I don't kill Honored Ones."

"But you do hold them prisoner," he pointed out.

"No one's a prisoner here," I said. "We brought you to our camp to keep you alive. Think of yourself as a kind of guest. For now, just forget everything else and concentrate on recovering. You've had a near brush with death."

"I feel like it," he admitted. "You're sure I'm not dying?"

"Positive," I lied. "Try and think of something besides the pain. Tell me about yourself. You know my name, but I've yet to learn yours."

"Sorry, I didn't think of it. I'm Terrac of Deep Pool. That's a settlement near Three Hills in Cros, a long way from here. Honored Thilstain and I were on the road for weeks to get this far."

His words cut off abruptly as he sucked in a great breath at what I supposed must be a particularly sharp throb of pain. It was a moment before he was able to continue with, "The Honored One goes to Whitestone on pilgrimage, while I journey there to join the priesthood, as was my father's dying wish. Everyone said if my mother were living, it would have been her wish as well."

He gasped those last words out in short, panting breaths. As I heard him grinding his teeth against the pain, I hesitated to ask what was on my mind. But I needed to know.

"You're not already a priest then?" I asked.

"Not yet, but Thilstain was instructing me."

This isn't good news, I thought uneasily. "I advise you to keep that fact to yourself," I told him. "The outlaws spare you for the sake of your priesthood. If they learn you're not an Honored, they'll have no compunction at killing you."

"An upright man doesn't lie," he pompously informed me.

"Then that man sets little store by his life," I answered. But sensing he was going to remain stubborn on the issue, I switched to a more persuasive tone. "Besides, you don't have to lie exactly. The assumption has already been made. It would be enough simply to hold your peace and let folk believe what they will."

His tone was hesitant. "But that's little different from a lie."

"What does it matter?" I demanded, losing patience. "What's one small lie to a lot of cutthroats anyway? Give them the truth and they'll kill you for thanks."

The boy either lacked the will to argue further or he couldn't summon the breath to do so.

"You should rest now," I said. "But think on what I've told you. I haven't gone to all this trouble only to see you kill yourself as soon as you get a chance to open your mouth."

"I am grateful to you," he said humbly. "I've much to thank you for."

"Forget it. Do you need anything?"

He asked for a drink of water, so I crept off to the nearby pool, filled a skin with the cool, clear water from the falls, and brought it back to him. After drinking thirstily, he quickly sank into an exhausted slumber.

The next day, noise and activity were kept to a minimum around camp to afford quiet for Dradac. I doubt anyone even remembered Terrac, the boy priest, unless they looked up to see me slithering in and out of the shelter all day, waiting on his needs.

He fared even worse today, waking rarely and only for short lengths of time. He gave no sign he remembered me or last night's conversation. He moaned and tossed around until he finally tore his stitches open and I had to fetch Javen to repair them. I felt relief each time the injured boy sank down again into a fitful rest.

It was a long day for me because my charge lacked strength to do anything for himself. I fed him, coaxed sips of water down his throat, and changed his bandages. Come nightfall, I was exhausted as I lay down to sleep. As I sprawled on the hard-packed earth beside his sleeping form, a numbing chill stole over the ground. Scooting over to press my back against the still, warm body beside me, I fell asleep wondering what would become of Terrac of Deep Pool and whether or not he would prove worth my efforts.

The following morning, Brig returned and from the moment he strode into camp, things began to improve. He took over the larger share of the work in nursing Terrac and looked impressed with what I had done for him. He didn't ask for details on how the priest boy came under my care and I didn't offer them, knowing he wouldn't approve of my having been placed in such a volatile situation, where it might easily had been me injured instead of the others.

Under Brig's care, Terrac's health steadily improved. Soon the day came when, with assistance, he could drag himself out of the dark hut and into the sunshine. Brig and I propped his back against the sun-warmed rock at the cave's entrance and he would sit there, face tilted toward the sky, for hours at a time. I couldn't tell if he was engaged in some sort of priestly meditation or just resting.

At first, he seemed uncomfortable when his fellow invalid, Dradac, began joining him. I couldn't see what he had to be disturbed at. The giant would only sit quietly by his side, making feeble attempts at whittling one handed, while letting his bad shoulder soak up the sun's rays. Javen assured the giant he would regain the use of his arm, but the healing process was going to be slow.

Over the next few weeks, Terrac came to accept Dradac's company and the giant became one of the few exceptions to Terrac's general rule of contempt for the outlaws. Brig, too, earned a measure of respect, probably for having cared for him during his convalescence, and even I was tolerated in a condescending but not terribly hostile way. However, it quickly became apparent no one else would be fortunate enough to penetrate Terrac's favored circle.

CHAPTER SIX

SPRINGTIME LENGTHENED INTO SUMMER AND the nights grew warm, the days uncomfortably hot and sticky. As soon as Terrac had recovered enough I needn't fear for him any longer, I moved back into the cave. I had my own semi-private space there, a cozy alcove with the waterfall sheeting down one side to form a thin screen between the outside world and me. I didn't mind the dim light or the lack of space. At this time of year, the slight dampness on the walls and floor was pleasant and I could roll over and stretch my hand out to touch the splashing fountain as it cascaded downward. The cool water was refreshing on hot nights.

But Terrac couldn't be persuaded to move into the cave with the rest of us. Even when the brown needles fell away from his flimsy, pine bough shelter, leaving only a naked frame of bare branches, he remained outdoors. I think it was the company inside he objected to. I was discovering he had a definite sense of superiority over the rest of us and I teased him this was unbecoming in a boy destined for priestly vows. He only sniffed unapologetically and cajoled me into helping him contrive a sturdier hut beneath the trees.

One morning, only a few days after the building of the new hut, Terrac and I were crouched together along the bank of the stream bordering camp. He was looking on with squeamish disgust as I gutted a rabbit for our breakfast when Rideon approached.

The brigand captain glared down on Terrac and stated his object without preamble. "It has come to my notice that you are able to move about again, boy."

Terrac nodded cautiously. I could see he was nervous in the outlaw's presence but striving to hide it.

Rideon said, "If that's the case, it appears the time has come for you to make a decision. I'm going to lay two choices before you. There is no third alternative, so don't ask for one. Give an answer I don't like and the question will be taken from your hands altogether. Understand?"

Terrac swallowed. "I suppose so."

"Good. These are your options. Firstly, you can swear on your honor to forever make your home in Dimmingwood with us. You'll earn your keep here with menial tasks around the camp, same as Ilan does, and never set foot beyond the borders of the forest again."

Terrac's eyes widened in alarm and I could see him forming a refusal, but Rideon didn't allow him time to get out the response. "Or," the outlaw continued, "should that idea not appeal to you,

you may choose the second alternative—refusing to take the oath and thus being put to a quick death. Priest boy or not, my generosity extends only so far and I won't risk a large-mouthed brat wandering loose to tell my enemies exactly where to hunt down my band."

I held my breath waiting for Terrac to say something foolish and he didn't disappoint me.

"You don't seem to care that the oath you're asking of me will change my life's plans," he protested.

Rideon shrugged. "I wasn't aware I was advocating one option over the other. I'm merely here to accept the first choice or to execute the latter, should it be your preference." He tapped the blade at his side for emphasis. "The ultimate decision is entirely yours."

Terrac flicked a frightened glance at the black blade, drew a deep breath, and appeared to startle even himself with the words that spilled from him. "I swear on my life and honor that I'll never leave the boundaries of this wood as long as I breathe. Not without the express permission of the outlaw, Rideon the Red Hand."

Rideon was the only one of us who appeared unsurprised. "A reasonable decision, priest boy. If ever you should rethink it, my blade and I will be on hand." He flashed his teeth in a grim smile and left us.

Terrac immediately looked miserable and I suspected he was thinking of how, with a few short words, he destroyed his hopes of entering the priesthood. In an attempt to cheer him I said, "It isn't so bad, you know. Maybe you'll come to like it here. And at least you're alive, which is more than anyone would've expected on the day you came."

He didn't look much comforted.

Later that day, I was kneeling beside Dradac, who was helping me repair an old knife that had lost its handle, when the heavy scuff of approaching boots alerted me to another arrival. Without looking up, I sensed it was Brig.

In a moment, his voice confirmed it.

"Is it true, Dradac?" Brig demanded angrily, ignoring my presence. "I've had my suspicions since the spring, but what I've heard from Nib today confirms it. Was Ilan with you when you confronted those travelers and nearly had yourself killed?"

My stomach lurched. I'd always known it was only a matter of time before he discovered the extent of my involvement in the episode that brought Terrac to us and I had an idea there would be trouble when that information surfaced. I just hoped I wouldn't be present for it. It was good my face was turned away from Brig then because I was sure my guilt was clearly written in my expression.

Dradac affected innocence. "What's this? Who said she was there?"

"Did you imagine I'd need to be told?" Brig asked. "I run up to Molehill for a few days and return to find an injured boy priest encamped in our midst and Ilan fluttering around his sick bed. Who else would have spared him?"

Dradac said, "What makes you so certain it wasn't me? Do you think I would murder a helpless boy wearing the robe of an Honored One? Imagine how many years bad luck that'd bring me."

"Drop the pretense. You're only making me angrier," said Brig.

The giant sighed. "All right, I confess. She was with me when we got the signal about the trespassers, so I let her come along to meet them. I wasn't planning to expose her to any real danger. But they appeared a harmless group and I thought it would be an exciting experience for her. There. Are you happy now I've admitted to my miscalculation?"

His easy smile faltered under Brig's silent scowl. "Now don't start growling at me, old bear. I didn't let any harm come to her. If it makes you feel better, I promise, when I'm recovered, I'll seek your approval before taking her out again."

"I've half a mind to see you never recover at all. What right did you think you had dragging a child into a situation where she might have been killed? It could easily have been her shot through with that bolt instead of you. How would you feel then?"

"Probably a good deal better than I do now," the giant joked. "Anyway, I just thought it was time Ilan had some practice dealing with these little situations. Part of the territory and all that. "

"From here on out, allow me to decide what lessons will be of use to her and when. Ilan knows she's supposed to avoid strangers in the wood and keep out of trouble."

Here I felt his accusing eyes burning into the back of my head, but, annoyed at being spoken over as if I had no say in this matter, I bit my tongue and refused to apologize.

"I'm sorry you don't appreciate my input, friend," Dradac was saying. "But I'm afraid I'm going to have to disagree with you on the point of what's best for Ilan. She's growing up faster than you realize and is learning to fend for herself. You're doing her a disservice if you won't allow her a little adventure once in awhile."

Brig sputtered, but I shot Dradac a grateful look.

In the end, we settled the matter with a compromise. It was determined I was to be given more freedom in the future, but this hinged on the condition that Brig wished me to improve myself in certain areas. He had taken up a strange notion I needed what he called "scholarly learning," although neither he nor anyone else in our band had ever possessed anything of the sort. I readily agreed to this, confident I was getting the best of the deal.

However, when I discovered a few days later exactly what he had in mind, I was no longer so sure.

I sat beneath a shady tree, a smooth plank of wood across my knees for a table. A yellowed sheet of parchment rested beneath the tip of my hovering quill. Terrac crouched behind me, leaning a little over my shoulder to observe my efforts. The quill's ink skipped and spattered irregularly as I attempted to copy out the letters Terrac had set down across the upper half of the page. At Terrac's direction, Brig had fashioned the writing implement from a quail feather and Brig and Terrac together had made the ink from the juice of wild berries. The parchment was a contribution from one of the outlaws. It had been confiscated from the hands of a reluctant scribe two seasons past and the thief had no use for it.

I silently cursed that outlaw now and the scribe before him. For an hour of every day I was forced to practice my letters, under Terrac's guidance. I knew Brig well enough to be sure he would see to it that I always had that hour to spare. He'd been pleased to learn Terrac had been taught to read and write by Honored Thilstain and quickly insisted the boy's learning be passed on to me.

"No, that's not it," Terrac said with a frown, snatching the pen from my fingers. "You've still got it wrong. Your lines should curve at the bottom—like this." He demonstrated and returned the implement to me.

As usual, he didn't complain or scold me for my slow fingers and slower wits, but his patience only served to irritate me further. I didn't know how Brig had threatened or cajoled him into tutoring me, but I was certain he could be enjoying the experience no more than I. I was well aware I made a sorry pupil. In fact, I wouldn't have blamed Terrac if he beat his head against a tree, in frustration, by the end of our hour, but for some reason he never did. The fact that he never laughed at the pitiful results of my effort only served to aggravate me further. I was sure he knew that and derived a twisted satisfaction from it.

After contemplating the untidy marks on the parchment before me, I threw my pen down in disgust. "Can't we just forget this and tell Brig I did the work?" I asked.

Terrac didn't blink at my outburst. I decided he was growing used to them.

"Of course not," he responded absently. "That would be lying. Now look, I think your trouble is how you keep confusing the first and third letters. They look alike but are a little different."

"Oh, I forgot priests don't lie," I mocked, ignoring his direction. "A simple untruth would probably torment your conscience for all time."

He regarded me with puzzlement and I realized he had no idea what I was talking about. I sighed and asked myself how I was going to endure another million lessons like this one. My companion was so good and patient he grated unintentionally on my every nerve. Or at least most of the time I believed it was unintentional. I doubted he possessed an ounce of spite in him. His only character flaw was his habit of frowning down his nose at everyone who failed to meet his standards, but even this snobbery seemed unconscious. At times, I asked myself why I had saved him at all. Then I would grudgingly recall those rare occasions when we actually had a good time together, those days when we explored the forest, swam in Dancing Creek, or hunted stink snakes in Heeflin's Marsh at Dimming's edge.

But today I was in no mood for such charitable memories. "Why do you even do this?" I demanded impatiently. "I'm hopeless at these letters! You can't enjoy teaching me. Not unless you derive pleasure from laughing secretly at my mistakes. You shouldn't allow Brig to force you into it. You always do whatever you're told and no one respects you for it. No one but me even likes you."

"They don't?" He sounded confused and slightly hurt, but I didn't care.

"No, they don't. They laugh at you to your face and you take it like a dumb animal."

He looked thoughtful. "Honored Thilstain taught me it was a priestly duty to be humble, to seek peace and to serve all."

I snorted. "I can't even imagine how little pride you must have," I said.

He looked wounded. I could see his mind working as he struggled to form the right reply, but I gave him no opportunity to voice it. I was in a difficult mood and I felt it wouldn't require much provocation for me to take my frustration out on him. He was a slight figure, still frail after his recovery, and I was sure I could knock him into tomorrow without expending much effort. "I'm leaving now," I said in a tone that brooked no argument. "You can tell Brig whatever you want."

"But your lesson!" he protested, dismayed. "Brig swore he would beat me senseless—"

"So stand and take it," I said unsympathetically. "I think you owe it to me. Have you forgotten how I nursed you back from the brink of death? And I pretty nearly saved your life again only the other day when you almost drowned in Dancing Creek. You were thrashing around, crying out for help, and no one else came running. But did I throw you a stone?"

"No, but—-"

"No, indeed, I didn't." I answered my own question. "I leapt straight in and dragged you from the water at no small risk to my life and limb."

"Life and limb?" he cried incredulously. "You're taller than I! The water scarcely reached to your neck!"

I shrugged. "Can't blame that on me. Maybe *you* should've been the girl."

His face reddened and he surprised me by kicking the wooden writing slab off my lap. "You want a fight?" he demanded, voice squeaking in fury. "Is that what you're looking for?" He doubled his fists and took a fighting stance.

I couldn't hide my amusement. I'd never seen him in such a temper.

"Think you can fight, do you, boy?" I looked up, startled, at the voice that belonged to none other than the Red Hand himself. Where had he come from? We were in an out of the way spot and I hadn't heard his approach. I stirred uneasily, wondering what he wanted. I could see his presence unnerved Terrac.

"We weren't fighting," I assured Rideon. "Just playing around."

"Ah, I see. Play-fighting." Rideon's smile didn't reach his eyes. He turned his calculating gaze on Terrac. "Wouldn't you rather learn to fight for real?" he asked.

Terrac looked uneasy and I found myself feeling unexpectedly protective of him, so I broke in with, "He's a priest, Rideon. He cannot do violence."

The outlaw smirked, looking Terrac up and down. "A flimsy excuse," he said. "I won't have such a cowardly pup in my band. If he wants to live among us, let him learn to defend himself."

Terrac said, "With all due respect, I don't consider myself a member of your criminal band." There was a cold light in his eyes that, for a moment, drowned out the fear as he added, "But while I'm forced to live among you, I earn my way. I do my chores around camp and I work as hard as anyone."

I was surprised to find myself feeling a little proud of the boy. Grown men didn't argue with Rideon. Even so, I rushed to put a stop to his foolhardiness before he could talk his way into a thrashing or worse.

"He does work hard," I said. "But if you're of a

mind to see him fight, Rideon, I'm sure he wouldn't refuse. There's never any harm in learning to defend oneself." I cast a warning glance Terrac's way, willing him to keep silent. I could feel him burning to martyr himself, so it was a pleasant surprise when he held his peace.

Rideon scratched at the stubble on his chin. "Wise words, hound. Now I've a mind to see some sport, so let me see you practice between yourselves a bit. And to add to the challenge, the winner gets to spar with me as his reward. How's that?"

Terrac and I exchanged uneasy glances, but neither of us dared argue. I was sure Brig wouldn't approve of this, but he wasn't here. "It will be just until one of us downs the other," I reassured Terrac, who looked slightly ill. He appeared stunned by my acceptance.

Rideon put in mockingly, "Come now, priest boy. You're not afraid to fight a girl, are you?"

That seemed to decide Terrac. "Very well, if I must." He agreed, jutting his chin out defiantly and pushing up his sleeves. "What are the rules of this game?"

"No rules, no game," Rideon said. "Just pound one another until one of you can no longer stand."

Terrac's eyes narrowed disapprovingly, but he offered no argument. "All right then. Let's get this over with," he said. Even crouching with fists drawn, he didn't look very convincing. Every rigid line of his body betrayed his reluctance.

I stepped in and doubled my own fists, feeling

as unenthusiastic as he looked. It was hardly an even match. Despite the nearness of our ages, I had a good six inches on Terrac and I'd had years of outdoor labor to strengthen my muscles. It also wasn't long ago that he'd been deathly ill. I resolved to go as easy on him as I could, but I wouldn't let him win. Instinctively, I felt this was some sort of test of Rideon's and that the outcome might make a difference in my future.

I guess I allowed myself to be distracted by my thoughts for I was suddenly brought back to the moment by a hard fist jabbing me in the ribs. From a grown man, such a punch would have been painful. From Terrac it was more like a sharp poke. Still, it allowed me to fight back without feeling guilty. My answering swing fell wide as Terrac dodged with surprising dexterity, throwing me off balance. The next two punches caught me in the face. I bit my tongue and that hurt more than the actual blows. It also made me realize I needn't concern myself so much with going easy on my opponent after all.

As I spat blood, I could hear Rideon laughing behind me. Terrac's eyes were apologetic, but that didn't stop me from feeling a rush of anger that he was making me appear a fool before my captain. I launched an all-out assault against him, throwing a series of punches he couldn't move quickly enough to block. I kept up my attack, but the priest boy refused to fall no matter how mercilessly I punished him.

He gave up ground readily enough, until we had backed out of the clearing and found ourselves fighting knee-deep in bramble bushes. I no longer knew who I beat or why, so intent was I on winning. I hardly noticed my weariness or my skinned knuckles. I was close to victory; I could feel it. As Terrac stumbled backward against a log, I seized the opportunity to drive a blow into his belly. He staggered and doubled over. Although I knew it was cheap, I followed the punch with a knee to his face. That knocked the strength from him and he dropped.

Upon seeing him downed, my anger instantly evaporated, leaving exhaustion and guilt in its wake. I leaned forward to grip my knees and catch my breath. Then I extended a hand to help Terrac to his feet. He accepted it with barely a sign of hesitation. It wasn't in his character to hold a grudge. Still, I felt a twinge of shame, noting his swollen lip and the bruises already forming over his cheekbones.

He seemed to sense my thoughts. "It's all right," he told me quietly. "Perhaps I'll do as much for you one day."

I accepted the threat as my due and turned my attention to freeing myself from the clinging bushes, as Rideon approached. When my captain stood before me, I believed he had come to see how badly I was hurt. I was relieved of that misapprehension when, without word or warning, he suddenly dealt me a ringing blow to the jaw.

Stunned, I reeled backward to the ground. I thought he would wait for me to get back to my feet. He didn't. Instead he battered me with a series of vicious kicks, the strength of which knocked the breath from me. I sensed the futility of attempting escape and instead curled my body into a ball, wrapping my arms around myself to deflect the worst of the blows.

My pitiful reaction appeared to enrage Rideon, for he launched a particularly rough kick into my face. Sparks exploded before my eyes and I felt my nose crunch. Face throbbing and nose filling with blood, I sucked in pained gasps of air through my mouth. It suddenly occurred to me the blows might not stop until I was dead, and for the first time, I was afraid. Inwardly, I clawed after my magic, but once I grasped it my mind was too clouded by the pain to think how to use it. The most I could do was simply cling to the inner fire, as I tried to fight down the rising darkness.

When the attack ceased as unexpectedly as it had begun, I knew a moment of intense relief. The outlaw must have expended his strength. Slowly, tentatively, I released my grip on the magic and let it slip away. Then I lifted a trembling hand to explore my aching face. My skin was slick to the touch, my nose crooked and swollen. Upper lip and jaw throbbed. Mentally, I categorized each pain: aching limbs, bruised body, and a fiery agony in my ribs. Rideon rolled me roughly onto my back. I tried to pry one bloodied eye open, but the lid remained stubbornly sealed. The other eye managed to open into a narrow slit, affording me a squinted view of my surroundings. The treetops swayed dizzyingly overhead. I was very near to blacking out and didn't fight it. The rest would've been a welcome relief.

"I'd say this has been a profitable exercise," Rideon announced with deliberate ease. "I'm sure you've both learned something."

I struggled to focus my watering eye on his shadowy figure looming over me, but my vision was oddly clouded. His voice was casual as he continued, "We will never make any great fighter of you, hound. That is sure. Has Brig never taught you, the larger the opponent the greater the courage you will need to defeat him?"

I was too miserable to construct a defense. I understood his implication—I was a disappointment. Feeling wretched and ashamed of my weakness, I watched him stride away. Then I raised a hand to my face, wincing at my careful touch. My nose felt as if it were swelling larger by the second.

Terrac suddenly appeared and helped me right myself. I couldn't stand yet, so I slouched where I was, panting through my mouth and dabbing at my bloody nose with my sleeve. I felt unreasonably angry with Terrac, crouched patiently at my side, for witnessing my humiliation. I hated his concerned expression as he peered into my battered face.

"I think only your nose is broken," he assured

me now. "The swelling and blood may make it hard to breathe for a while, but eventually it will mend itself."

"How does it look?" I asked. "Ugly?"

Terrac hesitated. "Not too ugly. I think it will be all right on you. Look at Illsman; a crooked nose just makes him seem tough."

I winced and tried to convince myself I didn't mind being compared to the ugly outlaw. No one would have taken a pretty female brigand seriously anyway. But I reached a decision. "I'm not going back to camp like this," I told Terrac.

He tried to protest. "But those cuts on your face need cleansing."

"You can do that for me here," I said firmly. I wouldn't be seen by Brig like this. Not after the recent argument between him and Dradac. I couldn't allow him to think he'd been right all along.

Terrac must have sensed my determination. "Very well," he said. "I'll run back and fetch a poultice from Javen for those cuts. I'll bring food also. It will be a few days before you're moving around much, and we'd go hungry if it were left for me to do the hunting."

"We?" I questioned.

"Yes, we. I'm not about to leave you out here alone after that plague-cursed animal has rendered you too battered to look after yourself."

"Don't speak of the Hand like that," I ordered halfheartedly. "He is Rideon. He can do whatever he pleases."

"*Can* isn't the same as *should,* but I won't argue the point. Wait here and I'll return as quickly as I can." He clambered to his feet.

"Say nothing to Brig," I warned as he left. "If he asks, say only that I plan to sleep out tonight. He knows I do that sometimes."

Terrac nodded briefly, although I could see he didn't appreciate being drawn into my deception. And that was how we came to make camp alone for three days.

CHAPTER SEVEN

A S SOON AS I WAS able to move, we shifted to a better location. I tried again to persuade Terrac to leave me, making no secret of the fact I would prefer to be without him. But the priest boy wouldn't budge. I suspected he secretly enjoyed witnessing my suffering. Over the following days, I treated him as harshly and as ungratefully as I knew how, but never was I able to sway him in his determination to share in my self-imposed exile.

That first night out of Red Rock, I was too sore to plan for anything in the way of shelter, so we slept beneath a row of shrubbery. With Terrac sleeping at my back, I was reminded of the nights we spent in our pine bough shelter last spring. Only then, it had been he who suffered. I didn't like the sense of our places being changed.

It rained that night.

The following day found the skies clear again. By mid-afternoon the sogginess had gone from the ground, but our clothing remained miserably damp throughout the day. We did very little except sitting about, sulking and arguing over whether we should return to Red Rock. In the end, I won out and we stayed. We fared better the next night because the weather was warm and dry. By this time I was in good enough condition the two of us were able to climb a stout tree to sleep in. We braced ourselves in the branches, where I passed a comfortable night, although Terrac still looked weary in the morning. He was unaccustomed to sleeping among the green leaves and said he scarcely closed his eyes all night for fear of falling to the ground in his sleep.

We consumed the last of our food on that second day. Terrac went off in search of more, but I lacked the inclination to join him. My mind was still on Rideon and my disgrace. It was no surprise when Terrac returned with nothing more than a handful of berries, although I had lent him my hunting knife. If I knew Terrac, he passed up all sorts of fox dens and rabbit holes because he hadn't the heart to kill anything. I had sunk into such depression I didn't even bother mocking him.

I hardly cared that I huddled down to sleep on an empty stomach that night, having let Terrac keep his scant meal to himself. They were bitter-berries, a fact I didn't bother sharing with him. Instead, I enjoyed a faint satisfaction each time I heard him wake during the night to vomit up the contents of his stomach. Those frequent interruptions made it difficult for me to find sleep, however. I lay half-reclined among the branches for a long time, staring into the shadows of the leaves overhead. As I listened to the creaks and rustles of the branches below and to the subsequent sounds of the priest boy disgorging his meal, I wondered how much longer I could hold out before giving up my wounded pride and returning to Red Rock. I tried to imagine what Brig and Dradac and the others would be doing back in camp right now. Eventually, I slipped off to sleep.

Gentle hands woke me to the cold, grey light of early dawn. It was still more night than day, and I didn't understand why I was being awakened so early. Mama bent over my pillow, the sweeping ends of her silvery hair brushing my face.

She whispered, "Come, little chickling. Don't make a sound." A strange excitement lit her eyes. I asked no questions but slipped out of bed, exclaiming softly as my small feet touched the cold, dirt floor. Mama pressed a warning finger to her lips, casting an anxious glance into the shadows across the room where Da slept.

She had already collected my things and now she moved silently, helping me slip a dress over my head and pull warm stockings up my legs. She was dressed to go out as well and over her shoulder she carried a canvas sack with a loaf of bread peeking out of its mouth. I was curious where we went in such a hurry it would be necessary to eat along the way, but I kept quiet.

There was urgency in Mama's eyes and in the

quick movements of her hands as she sat me on the floor and tugged on my ragged shoes. I scarcely had time to pull my feet under me again before she took me by the shoulders and guided me quickly through the semidarkness and out the doorway.

The farmyard, illuminated by the faint morning light, stood empty before us. I stole a glance back over my shoulder to where Da lay, snoring loudly in the big bed. Mama and I exchanged conspiratorial smiles as we silently abandoned the little cottage and slipped into the grey world outside. Mama transferred her grip to my hand and led me across the yard, away from the cottage. Stealthily, we veered behind the barn and into the shadow of the plum trees. I felt a surge of excitement because I sensed whatever was happening was forbidden and secret—an adventure.

We crossed the farmyard and topped the ridge, pausing to look down on the sleepy cottage below. Only then did I feel both our moods lighten. On the far side of the ridge lay the neighboring village, but Mama didn't lead me down that way. I had only a brief glimpse of the low cluster of flat roofs before we moved on. We climbed a steeper hill, then descended its slope into another valley, where a narrow road snaked along its base. Once we were on the road, Mama finally allowed me a slightly slower pace, but I still had difficulty matching her quick strides.

"It is a long way to Journe's Well," she told me apologetically. "We need to arrive before the sun is high." She gave no more explanation than that.

By the time the sky had changed from morning's grey to a pale blue, I had begun to miss my breakfast. Mama swung the sack around from her shoulder and broke off a chunk of bread for us both. We ate while we walked. Very soon after, my feet began to hurt. Mama lifted me onto her thin shoulders and carried me for a time, but we both soon wearied of that and I walked again.

Mama seemed to grow more agitated the farther we traveled. I sensed whatever mysterious adventure lay ahead frightened as much as it excited her. She began talking after a while, more to herself than to me. I comprehended little of her words. She told me we were making this trek to Journe's Well to catch a glimpse of the Praetor's soldiers, camped there on their journey back from the North. They had served the provinces for years, fending giants from our borders and were at last free to return home. These men, the Iron Fists, were the bravest soldiers of our province and were led by the son of the old Praetor himself, she explained.

I barely listened to her words. I couldn't see how the Praetor, his son, or their soldiers had anything to do with me. Why should I be interested in people I'd never met? Now, if any of the Praetor's men could ride Carp Wildtooth's meanest bull, well, that would be a thing worth hearing about.

We reached Journe's Well late in the morning. Although we didn't approach very near, I could see even at a distance that the camp bustled with *activity. Some men were striking tents and loading supplies onto horses and pack animals. Other soldiers were already mounting their horses. Mama told me they would march to Selbius today, where folk would line up in the streets to watch them pass. In the city, feasts would be thrown for a week to celebrate their return. This sounded very grand to me and I wished I could see it, but Mama said we could not journey so far today. She looked as if she regretted it as much as I did.*

Circling the camp, we kept at a distance. No one saw us or, if they did, they didn't care that their movements were spied on by a silver-haired peasant woman and a small child. There was an outcropping of rock at the base of a craggy hill overlooking the Well, and it was to this we moved, scaling the pile until we could look down on the evacuating camp without being observed.

Mama leaned forward, scanning the ground below. I wondered what she expected to find amid all the activity of rushing men and stamping horses. Then, "There," she muttered softly. Turning to me, she asked, "Do you see that man, chickling?" She directed my attention to a darkly handsome young man mounted atop a war steed. He had an aura of power that made him stand out from the other soldiers and his black armor and horse were finer than any of those around him.

I shivered, for the sight of the dark man touched something deep within me, awakening a fear I could find no cause for. At the moment I looked down on him his head was tilted back as he drank deeply from a water skin. At his heels a young lad sat a gray gelding and held aloft a pennant depicting a rearing black bear against a field of scarlet. I watched the soldier finish his drink and toss the skin to the boy. Then, as if suddenly sensing my eyes on him, the dark man looked up. I ducked out of sight, seized for a moment by the foolish fear he had read my thoughts, felt the curious connection between us that I did. But no, when I peered down on him again, he had already looked away.

"Did you see his face, little one?" Mama asked me.

I said I did, remembering that harsh profile with the tight mouth and long, hawkish nose.

"That man will be very great one day. I brought you here to look at him because he is going to be important in the future. Do you understand?"

I said I did because it was what she appeared to want. I wondered if she, too, felt the power I sensed emanating from the dark soldier. It was one of what she called her 'talents'—her magical abilities. She saw people's inner qualities—their hidden virtues and vices.

We remained hidden among the rocks for what felt like a very long time. I quickly grew bored and, when Mama wasn't looking, nibbled on bits of bread and cheese from our sack. The sun rose higher in the sky. It was hot, crouching where the bright rays beat down on the rocks. We didn't leave until the camp was emptied and the last of the dust *had settled after the soldier's horses. Then we crept down from our spot.*

As I clambered back down the rocks, I stepped on a patch of loose pebbles and slipped. Mama was too far ahead to catch me, so I fell, spilling headfirst down the hill. A sharp chunk of rock sliced my arm on the way. Then I hit the ground.

With a start I sat up in the darkness, nearly tumbling out of my tree.

"Mama?" I called. Of course she didn't answer. Had I really expected her to? I lifted my sleeve and felt the ridged scar along my forearm, where I'd clipped the rock during my tumble. It was an old injury and I'd never been able to remember how I'd gotten it. Until tonight.

I leaned back against the tree again and closed my eyes, attempting to shake my mother's image from my mind. I scarcely thought of her anymore. I felt uneasy, knowing she could still creep into my dreams after all this time. Was the magic trying to tell me something? I shook my head. That was ridiculous. The incident meant nothing. Neither Mama nor I had ever spoken again of our secret journey or of the dark man under the black-and-scarlet pennant. Strange that I should relive the incident now, but then I supposed it was no stranger than any of the other wild things folk dreamed about.

I tried to go back to sleep, but remnants of

the dream clung to my mind. The dark soldier's face was as fresh in my memory as if it were only yesterday I'd seen him. I wondered who he was and why he was important, and the wondering kept me awake the rest of the night. I had a growing conviction that if I could ever tie together the loose ends of all my scattered memories, I might make sense of the mysteries of my past.

As the early light of dawn crept over us, I decided I could bear it no longer. I reached below and awakened Terrac with a rough shake of the twin branches he sprawled over. He woke with a start, tumbling from his perch. Luckily, we weren't far from the ground and a convenient cluster of shrubbery saved him from a nasty landing. He wasn't too kindly disposed toward me after that and even less so when I told him why I'd stirred him. It was one of the few times I managed to ruffle his placid disposition.

"You wake me at dawn's first light and drop me from a tree so I can run and fetch for you?" he demanded in disbelief.

"I need the parcel now," I explained patiently. "I've told you how to retrieve it and I don't intend to waste the morning arguing, so away with you. And be quick about it or I'll be forced to set you in your place. Again."

Waving a dismissive hand in the direction of Red Rock, I lay back in my lofty perch to gaze into the leafy green branches above. A pinecone was lobbed past my head, but I ignored it.

My companion grumbled, a low string of phrases unworthy of a priest, but eventually the crackle of sticks and the rustle of underbrush told me he was walking away. I wondered absently if he would bother to return, then decided even if he didn't, at least I was finally rid of him.

It was hours before I saw him again. He still had a grim set to his mouth and an offended air about him as he set the required parcel at the base of the tree and shouted up that if I wanted it, I could come down and get it.

Ignoring his injured attitude, I scrambled down, snatching up the leather-wrapped package.

"What took you so long?" I demanded. "Get lost along the way?"

"Yes," he said sullenly. "You knew I would. I can't tell one of these rotten trees from another."

I sat down, my back against the tree trunk, to unwrap my bundle. Stripping away the oiled strips of leather I had wrapped it in for protection, I held the brooch in my hands. When I flipped it over, the tiny letters etched across the back looked just as I remembered them. They seemed less strange to me now that I had practiced writing a bit myself, but I was still not familiar enough with the letters to sound them all out. Irritated, I thrust the brooch at my companion. "Here. Tell me what this says."

"I won't," he said. "Read it yourself."

"You know I cannot," I answered testily.

"I know that you could learn if you wanted to badly enough."

"But at this moment I cannot," I emphasized, as if speaking to a child. "You already read, while for me it will take months, if not years, to learn." I shook the brooch at him. "This pin was given me by my dead mother, who claimed it held the secret to protecting me. Maybe this writing will give me some clue as to what she meant."

He folded his arms, unmoved. "Then you'd better start attending your lessons. Now there's something you're suddenly eager to read, you'll work twice as hard at your letters. Coincidentally, as Brig grows impatient with your lack of progress, your renewed efforts will spare me a beating from him. Let us consider that to be your good deed for the year."

"I'm not the priest," I reminded him sourly.

"Neither am I. Or have you forgotten?"

"Yes," I said. "You lie so convincingly it's easy to forget the truth."

I saw his confidence falter. "I don't lie," he said. "If I've allowed Rideon to mislead himself, it's only because I don't care to be murdered."

Before I could slip in a cutting remark, he changed the subject. "But never mind that. Let's speak of your problem. I'll make you a bargain. If you're willing to redouble your efforts and pay attention to what I teach you, I promise I'll have you reading by winter. Come now, that isn't far off."

I leaned forward. "Now I'll make you an offer. You tell me right this moment what the writing on the brooch says or I'll tell Rideon you're not really a priest."

Terrac winced but held his ground. "Tell Rideon I'm not a priest and I'll tell everyone how he knocked the feathers out of you."

I knew he was waiting to bring that up. I sank back in defeat. "You win, priest boy." I conceded ungraciously. What choice did I have? Terrac was a fair teller of tales and too honest to skim over details. I knew by the time he finished the story, I'd be a laughing stock around the outlaw camp.

"Good," he said now. "We'll give up this sulking nonsense and return to Red Rock first thing tomorrow morning, where we will resume your lessons."

Too dispirited to object, I nodded dumbly, returned the brooch to its protective leather wrapping and tucked it into my tunic.

But as it turned out, we didn't wait for the following morning to return to Red Rock. Brig found us that very afternoon. The purposeful way he strode into our little camp told me he hadn't found us by accident. I ground my teeth. Obviously, Terrac had talked to him. I should have known better than to send the priest boy back to camp for the brooch. Brig stood silently before us and looked me up and down.

"Sorry," Terrac mumbled. "He caught me and threatened to beat it out of me. He knew something was wrong when you stayed away so long."

I could see by Brig's lack of reaction to my battered face that he already knew what happened. Yet another thanks I owed Terrac. I was relieved at least when he asked no questions.

"Let us see the damage, Ilan," he said, turning my face to examine the bruises. "Nothing serious," he observed. "But you should've come back earlier and let me clean up these little cuts. For that matter, you'd have done better to avoid a fight with the Hand in the first place. Still, a beating is nothing to be ashamed of. Sulking about it, though, that's another matter. Hiding away from camp only makes you look like a weakling." It stung that Brig, of all people, would kick me while I was down. That was why I said, "You ran away to hide in the forest when your Netta left you and took your sons. Maybe that's why she went— she didn't want to be married to a coward. I'm not surprised you've nothing to say to me about standing up for myself in a fight but criticize me instead for failing to run from one. When have you ever stood your ground for anything?"

Even as I said it, the unwanted memory flashed through my mind of Brig withstanding Rideon's orders to protect a little orphaned girl. Right away I could have bitten my tongue out, but it was too late to call the words back.

Brig's eyes flashed with a mixture of anger and pain. I thought if he hit me I would deserve it. I heard Terrac clearing his throat and backing away. But Brig wasn't going to let me off so easily.

He took a long breath and it was a moment before he spoke.

"You've developed a sharp tongue, Ilan," he observed quietly. "I think I liked you better when you were that silent little hound."

Filled with remorse, I tried to apologize. "I'm sorry, Brig. I don't know why I said that. It wasn't true."

He held up a hand. "Never mind. If you feel you owe me an apology, you can make it up by coming back to camp. Stop skulking around out here like a petulant child I have to be ashamed of."

"Alright." My voice was heavy with regret, but if Brig noticed, it didn't soften him. Terrac and I followed him back to Red Rock where I faced an unpleasant handful of days to follow.

The bruises on my face attracted a certain amount of attention back at camp and a few of the outlaws asked if I'd stuck my face into a badger's den. I told myself they meant no harm with their jokes and that for every man who remarked on my battered countenance, there were just as many who appeared not to notice it at all. Still, I knew everyone had heard my story and that was deeply humiliating.

I avoided Terrac during this time. Although I knew he hadn't meant any ill in betraying me to Brig, I couldn't shake the notion none of this would have happened if not for him. Of course I realized I couldn't keep away from him forever. Sooner or later I must stick to our agreement about the lessons. But how could I do that when I couldn't abide the sight of him anymore? My anger at him grew and the strength of it only made me more miserable. I had grown accustomed to his odd, deprecating company and now I found myself strangely lonely without him.

As for the Hand, he treated me as if nothing had ever happened. It stung to think my captain could dismiss me so quickly after his former harsh treatment, but I told myself it was for the best. I would keep out of his way until another opportunity to prove myself came along. Then I wouldn't fail him.

Out of all the worries preying on my mind over the following days, my disagreement with Brig loomed largest. Since our heated words, he didn't seem to look at me in the same way. I couldn't say he treated me unkindly. But there was something missing from our friendship that had always been there before. I felt I no longer had his trust.

CHAPTER EIGHT

TIME PASSED AND MY FOURTEENTH birthday came and went with little to mark it. It wasn't the true date of my birth anyway, but the day Brig and I had chosen to celebrate it, as I could never recall the real one. The two of us used to pass this day in some pleasant way, with the cooking of a favorite treat or the giving of a small gift. Other times, we might simply spend the day together, hunting in the forest or visiting one of the little woods villages. But this year, neither of us mentioned the occasion.

My lessons with Terrac resumed. Brig finally noticed I was avoiding them and put an abrupt stop to it. This time I set to work with an interest born of determination, promising myself I would soon be able to decipher the writing on my mother's brooch. At first, I held on to my resolution not to speak to the priest boy, but it was difficult to ignore someone you had to be close to for an hour out of every afternoon. Inevitably, the day came when he asked me a question about my lesson and I unthinkingly responded. As easily as that, the feud between us was broken.

My eagerness to learn made a vast difference in the progress of my lessons. The day arrived when I began writing short words and soon after that, I was spelling my own name. Even then, Terrac suggested I continue with our sessions until my skills had grown as far as possible. I enthusiastically followed his advice, for I was discovering in myself something unexpected. I enjoyed learning.

One afternoon I presented Brig with a gift: his name inscribed in large, neat letters on a sheet of parchment.

"And what do you expect me to do with this, wear it about my neck like a sign?" he asked gruffly, his needle barely pausing as it flew in and out of a tunic he was mending.

But I had seen the look of wonder on his face as he contemplated the letters I had set out. Here was I, one he had raised from a child, doing a thing that in all his years he had never learned. Only pretending to look away, I watched from the corner of my eye as he carefully folded the page and tucked it away for safe keeping. His unspoken pride meant more than I could tell. I felt that a brick had been laid, that day, in bridging the gap between us.

Not long after that, Dradac came to me and asked if I'd like to help him out on his road to recovery. His shoulder had healed nicely where he'd taken the crossbow bolt, but Javen said if he wanted to regain full use of his arm, he would need to exercise it often. I was pretty sure this was partially an excuse on the part of the giant to teach me combat skills without upsetting Brig. Either way, I was happy to comply and we settled on the early morning as a good time to begin our exercises.

The following dawn couldn't come quickly enough for me. I rose with the sun, breakfasted early, and went out into the morning chill to wait beside the stream for Dradac. This ritual became a familiar one in the weeks to follow. The redheaded giant was never there when I arrived and I would sit on the dew sprinkled grass by the water's edge to wait.

I quickly found Dradac to be a more difficult master than I'd supposed. With his one undamaged arm, he made a more formidable opponent than most men with two sound ones, and he shed his usual, easygoing temper during our practice sessions, so that I sometimes felt I was facing a dangerous stranger instead of an old friend. I realized he wanted me to take this training seriously for my own good, but even so, I was truly stunned on that first morning by the number of times he seized me by the collar and dunked me into the cold pool to 'wake me up.' His strength was unsurprising for a man of his size, but more than that, he was quick. I soon learned just how quick as we progressed to mock fighting with knives.

Even with the blades dulled, by week's end, I had shallow cuts and bruises stretching halfway up my arms and even one or two across my face. Dradac believed in teaching by experience and much as it unnerved me to see him flying at me with whizzing blades, I had to admit it did give me incentive to learn quickly. He was always watching me, forever on the lookout for signs of weakness. I had no idea how I was standing up to his expectations.

The sword wasn't Dradac's best weapon, but we worked with those too. I had learned enough by then to know what it was to have a particular aptitude for a certain style of fighting and it was easy to discern how much more comfortable the giant was with a staff or pair of knives than a long blade. Nevertheless, he was skilled enough to defend himself competently with one, which was more than I could say for myself in the beginning.

I was surprised one afternoon to find Terrac skulking around the edges of our training ground as we practiced. Dradac let him watch us for a few minutes. Then, pausing from sparring with me, he wiped a trickle of sweat from his brow.

"Terrac," he called. "Why don't you come and practice with Ilan for a bit? Just until I've caught my breath."

Terrac hesitated only a moment before nodding mutely and stepping forward. Dradac decided, with two inexperienced fighters, it would be advisable to trade real blades for the bundled lathes we kept on hand but rarely used. He pressed one into Terrac's hands, showing him how to grasp it properly, while

I snagged another for myself. Then, standing back, he nodded for us to proceed.

As the match began, I tried to go easy on Terrac, remembering how ashamed I'd been after Rideon had forced me to injure him. Pacing circles around the clearing, we parried and blocked one another's thrusts for a short time. Then, seeing he was working up a sweat and that his hands were beginning to tremble from the unaccustomed weight of the lathe, I felt a stirring of sympathy. That was why I dropped my defense and allowed him to tap me across the chest. It was hard not to laugh because he did it so gently, like he was swatting a fly that had landed on me.

"Killing stroke," Dradac called out and Terrac and I lowered our lathes. I thought Terrac would be pleased, but, instead, he was frowning as the giant stepped forward to reclaim his weapon.

"Another round?" Dradac offered. "You were doing well."

Terrac shook his head. "Batting at one another with sticks like a pair of angry children holds little appeal for me," he said. He offered us a good afternoon and walked away.

"What's wrong with him?" I demanded. "He looked at me like I was a piece of itchleaf in his pants."

"The next time you fight, make an honest attempt," Dradac said. "Nobody likes to win by default. Nobody worth beating, least ways."

After that, Terrac came regularly to our

sessions. He wasn't present every day, but he showed up often enough that he developed a fair skill at fighting with the lathes and, later, with real blades. Soon he was even besting me occasionally. I found myself enjoying those lessons.

I grew, both physically and in my capabilities, during that time. Even Terrac was no longer the scrawny weakling I remembered from our first meeting. His shoulders broadened and, as he continued growing, it became obvious he would soon be taller than I, a fact that disturbed me to no end. All the same, he still relied on me for the protection of my sharp tongue, if not that of my fists.

One afternoon, the two of us climbed together to the top of the highest rocks of Boulders Cradle, where we looked down on the expanse of treetops spreading below. I had worked up a sweat on the climb and now I was enjoying the feel of the cool wind drying the sweat on my skin. Lying on my belly near the edge, I looked down the way we had come. A small herd of deer was moving cautiously through the trees below. One moment I caught a glimpse of a tail or an antler through the leaves and in the next the view was lost as the animal moved into the shadows. I said to Terrac, squatting silent beside me, "You know, if we had a bow handy and I was a fair shot..."

Terrac snorted. "You'd have to be better than fair. The greatest marksman ever known couldn't take one of them down at this distance. You'd just waste a lot of arrows and try to make me go and find them."

"Maybe so, maybe not," I said, but I gave up watching the deer. Rolling onto my back, I stared up at the fat clouds drifting so low overhead I felt I could reach out and touch them. "The Hand says you never know what you have in you until you're pushed to your limit."

"The Hand," Terrac said and rolled his eyes. "I don't need the likes of him for inspiration." He stretched out on the stone beside me. "The rock's hard," he complained, squinting up at the sun. "And it's too bright up here."

"You know, you're going to have to toughen up if you're planning on living in the woods the rest of your life. Otherwise, you've a long time ahead to be miserable."

"Who says I'm staying forever?" he mumbled, putting one arm up to shade his eyes. "I haven't forgotten the priesthood."

"Rideon says so," I reminded him. "He'll never release you from your oath."

He didn't say anything, but I sensed his unhappiness. "Look," I offered in a rare moment of sympathy, "I think you make things harder on yourself than they have to be. The men would get used to you in time if you'd just try to belong. Prove your abilities to them and they'll respect you."

"Just what I've always yearned for," he said. "The respect of a filthy band of thieves and murderers. There's deep ambition."

I ignored his sarcasm. "Rideon's no mere thief—" I started to argue.

"Why does everything have to be about Rideon with you?" he asked. "The Hand says this; the Hand thinks that. I suppose if Rideon threw himself down from this rock like a madman, you'd follow him?"

I didn't have to think about it. "Of course."

"Have I mentioned before how pathetic your devotion is?" he asked.

"A couple of times. Mention it again and it'll be you testing the fall from here."

He frowned. "I can tell you something about Rideon," he said. "He didn't get to where he is by trotting blindly along at another fellow's heels. If you dream of ever being anything more than his shadow—"

"I don't."

"—you should begin separating yourself from Rideon and making your own way. Pursue your own goals."

"Shut up, priest boy, and worry about your dreams, not mine. It seems you aren't in such a hurry to catch up to them." That effectively ended the conversation.

But all his talk of unattained goals had me thinking. That evening, back in Red Rock cave, I slipped a lantern down from the wall and carried it back to my sleeping nook behind the waterfall. Beneath the dim glow of the light, I probed my fingers into a deep niche in the wall, dusting aside the dirt and pebbles concealing the hiding place. I wiggled my fingers into the tight space until I managed to gain hold of a thin, flat object and drew it out into the light. Hands trembling in eagerness, I unwrapped the leather-bound packet and the brooch fell out onto the dusty floor.

Its hammered metal surface gleamed beneath the fitful flicker of the lantern and the copper and amber inlays reflected the light in warm reds and browns. The pin was almost large enough to fill my palm when I picked it up and because of its size I suspected it wasn't a woman's ornament but intended for a male wearer.

Flipping it over to examine the writing etched into the back, I knew a brief moment of panic, where all my newfound knowledge of letters flew from my mind and I felt I was looking again at meaningless squiggles. Then the tiny letters lined up in my vision and suddenly made sense. They spelled out two words. FIDELITY and SERVICE, the famed motto of the house of Tarius. The house of the Praetor.

I mused long over my discovery before eventually rewrapping the brooch and returning it to its hiding place. What I couldn't understand was how my humble mother had ever come to own a trinket once belonging to the Praetor or to someone in his family. Was it stolen? Given? Bought? Was the possession of it a danger to me, suggesting I had an affiliation with the widely hated Praetor Tarius? Or was it a form of protection from the Fists, as my mother appeared to have believed, an indication anyone harming the bearer harmed the house of Tarius? I suspected the answer depended on what company I found myself in.

Viewed in that light, I decided I would be wise to keep the brooch and its original owner a secret for the foreseeable future, even from Brig and Terrac. I returned the lantern to its place on the wall and curled up on my sleeping pallet, where I lay awake for a time, staring into the darkness. When at last I slept, I dreamed of being pursued through the night, chased by a darkness I sensed closing in around me but could never see.

CHAPTER NINE

———◦◦◦———

THE SEASONS TURNED AND BEFORE I knew it, I was another year older. Little else changed in my life, except my relationship with Brig. That was unpredictable these days, at times thawing briefly but always growing cold again. I had no desire to mend the rift, deciding I hardly needed the bearded outlaw now I was grown enough to care for myself. I broke his rules, flaunting my newfound freedom, and slipped calculated slights into our conversations for the amusement of onlookers. Brig's response was to avoid me and, when he could not do that, to eye me warily, like a strange dog that might bite.

I was thinking of this one chilly morning in early spring, as I crouched in the boughs of a thick elder tree, watching a small collection of men, wagons, and pack horses parade their way slowly down the Selbius Road. Undeterred by the temperature or the state of the thawing roads, travelers streamed through Dimming again on their way to Selbius or Kampshire and we were glad to see them on the move, for it had been a long winter. The coming of spring made the Praetor's Fists and their way patrol more active too, but they troubled us less of late, as they were caught up feuding with the savage Skeltai tribes along the provincial borders.

There was a soft rustle in the branches beside me as my companion, a youth named Kipp, shifted his position. He drew an arrow from his quiver but didn't notch it to his bowstring yet. A careful examination of the woods around us belied the impression we were alone. There were nearly a dozen others of us strung out along the tree line, ducking behind stumps and lying low beneath piles of brush and bracken. We didn't have the travelers outnumbered, but the better part of their party were children and old folk and we calculated we had more than enough men to quell any resistance they might offer. We'd been lurking here in the shadows for an hour, since Ladley had first brought us word which road our prey followed, and I had long ago grown impatient.

Now I shifted my weight, flexing the muscles in my cramped calves, as I counted heads in the train winding slowly into sight. Two wagons led the way, the first an open cart, the second a larger conveyance with a wooden frame arching over the top and a thin strip of canvas stretched over it. Several small heads ducked from beneath the roof of this wagon and a skinny dog trotted along in its wake. I summed up the two drivers, both old men, and the trailing handful of travelers on foot. Half of them were women or youngsters. Bringing up the rear of the procession walked a broad man in the now familiar grey robes of a priest of the Light, pulling along behind him a line of weary looking pack animals laden with bundles. Seeing the Honored One among them, I breathed a sigh of relief Terrac wasn't here to see us persecuting a priest. I could well imagine what he would say to that.

It appeared to me as I looked down on them that these miserable travelers could scarcely have anything worth robbing. Perhaps in our more desperate years this would have been a worthwhile catch, but these days, we rarely extended a hand toward such slender pickings. I observed as much to Kipp, who grinned.

"If Ladley says they're worth our while, that's good enough for me. He's got a woman in Coldstream who tipped him off these travelers would be passing through. Information from the woods villagers is usually good."

It was true. We had long ago formed an uneasy truce with a number of the surrounding woods villages, whose inhabitants weren't averse to passing us useful bits of information. We occasionally ventured into their settlements for supplies and as long as we didn't steal anything or stir up trouble, most villagers turned a blind eye toward stealthy strangers in deerskin.

Kipp continued. "You hear what Ladley says about this caravan? He's insisting some wealthy nobleman travels with them under the guise of a commoner to protect himself from that wicked band of thieves led by Rideon the Red Hand. Ladley claims this party comes from Black Cliffs in Cros. You imagine folk have heard of us all the way up there?"

I shrugged. "It's not so far from here. Terrac says his old village is only a couple weeks distant. Merchants and peddlers travel a lot between Selbius and the Cros cities and I guess they'd warn others, wouldn't they?"

Kipp emitted a low whistle. "Infamous in two provinces. How much longer do you suppose it'll be before the Praetor decides to take us seriously?"

I shushed him, even though the caravan was too far away to hear his noise. "I don't know." I pointedly kept my voice low. "But Rideon will know how to handle it if trouble comes our way. His wits are a match for any Fist's."

"Maybe so, but I've got a bad feeling about all this attention."

"I'll be keeping my mouth shut and leaving those things to the Hand," I said shortly. "You can start telling him how to run things if you want, but don't expect me to back you up."

"That's the last thing I'd expect, the way you lick his boots these days." He grinned as he said it, to show he only half meant the words.

He had a roguishly attractive smile. Funny, I was just starting to notice things like that. Even the once scrawny Terrac could be a pleasure to look at with his tunic off during sword practice.

I shook these distracting thoughts from my

mind and returned my attention to the approaching party. I scanned their faces and dress as they drew near, but if any of them was a wealthy noblemen in disguise, they didn't show it. Soon they were passing beneath us. Kinsley whistled the signal and we abandoned our hiding places to descend on the startled party. A woman screamed in fright and many of the male travelers started and looked close to crying out themselves as our band dropped suddenly into their midst.

A few folk were stupid enough to put up a fight—two had walking sticks and one a short dagger—but our men quelled their resistance in a matter of moments with little bloodshed. Rideon preferred we not injure our victims if we could avoid it. This wasn't sentimentality on his part; it just made sense to antagonize the Praetor as little as possible. I was glad of this rule, in view of the wailing little heads I saw poking out of the canvas-covered wagon.

We rounded up all our prisoners and ordered them to sit cross-legged on the ground. Brig and another man, Dannon, stood guard over them, clubs in hand and threatening to dash the brains out of anyone foolish enough to attempt escape. The remaining outlaws began sorting through the wagons, seizing anything of value, but I didn't join them.

From the first, I had dashed up to hold the line on the pack horses, before they could spook at the confusion and gallop off down the road. Now with one hand I loosed the knots holding the packs on the back of the first mare and began lowering the bundles to the ground. She was a cantankerous animal and made her mistrust of me obvious by sidestepping and tugging sharply to the full reach of her rope. I extended a hand to stroke her nose, but she drew back her lips and snapped dangerous yellow teeth at my fingers.

"Whoa. Easy there, lady." I flattered soothingly. She seemed unaffected by my wheedling and stamped her feet, rolling a wild eyeball at me.

"She's no lady. She's a wicked old tart, that one."

I jumped at the unexpected voice behind my ear. I tried to spin around but found myself suddenly snatched from behind, my arms pinned behind me. I kicked and wriggled desperately, cursing myself for my carelessness, but no amount of squirming could free me. My assailant's arm may as well have been a band of iron around my chest.

"Kindly cease struggling, child, or I will be obliged to poke you in the back with this dagger, little as such a brutish act would appeal to me."

I stiffened and ceased my struggles, feeling the sharp point digging into my back.

"That's a good fellow," the stranger said. "No need for violence, is there?"

I had no chance to respond. He raised his voice to shout at my comrades, who remained oblivious to my predicament. "Hold there, you thieving wretches. Stop what you are doing and take your greedy hands off those wagons. Let these good folk up, help them reload their possessions, and speed them on their way. Ignore my orders and I'll have no choice but to resort to force."

My comrades paused, looking around incredulously to see who issued such outrageous orders. Then the voice of Rideon's right-hand man, Kinsley, rose over the lull. "What is this now, Honored? I don't know how we missed you, but settle down, you're upsetting folk. No one's going to suffer harm so long as they cooperate, and that includes you. Now why don't you release our little Hound there? Looks a bit white in the face."

"No harm?" my captor demanded. "I doubt any of these people being robbed would agree with you, but we'll not debate that. Just free them, together with their belongings, or you will find yourselves short one of your number."

Kinsley frowned, turning to confer with Brig and a few others. The remainder of the men resumed their work, as if there had never been any interruption.

"You may as well know this is no good," I warned my captor. "With the exception of one or two of my friends, my life wouldn't buy you a pork pie from most of these men, let alone your freedom."

"Not to worry, young man. I am prepared to adapt to the situation as necessary. I have fought giants and Skeltai in my time, and I think I'm a match for a ragtag band of thieves."

Despite the confident words, he planted his blade a little more deeply into my back and tightened his hold around my chest. Then, startled, he glanced down to see exactly what his grip encircled.

"Upon my ashes," he exclaimed. "You're a woman. Or a girl, at least."

"A low rumor invented by my friends to plague me," I said.

"Is that right?" He surprised me by laughing. "Well, whether you call yourself one or not, you're still a young woman, and as a priest of the robe, I should ordinarily release you and apologize for the manhandling. Unfortunately, since my companions are in danger at the moment—or at least their goods are—you can see I'm in no position to do anything of the kind."

"If you did, I'd kill you," I growled. "Give me the chance and I'll have first stab at you."

"Mean spirited, eh?" He sounded amused. "In that case, I suppose we'll both just have to wait and reconcile ourselves to whatever comes."

I felt ridiculous standing there helpless, holding a private conversation with the stranger while my companions a few yards distant were engaged in a discussion of my fate. Brig had abandoned the prisoners and hastened over to join them.

"What are they dragging their feet about?" my captor demanded in my ear. "True, you aren't much of a prize, but one thinks they would have some dredges of loyalty."

I shook my head and wished he would quit talking to me. He wasn't doing this right. I determined not to speak to him anymore, until he either killed me or lent me the opportunity to do as much for him.

I couldn't hear the discussion playing out before us but could see Brig shaking his head angrily and knew he was arguing on my behalf. Kinsley was gesturing toward me, shrugging, and everyone else just looked confused. I had never felt so humiliated and burdensome in my life. I might have told the priest he had made an unlucky choice. He ought to have snatched a more popular captive.

But I didn't have to, for he seemed to read my mind. "I can see you have not exactly endeared yourself to your friends, young one. This grows awkward."

"You aren't the one looking foolish and helpless," I gritted out, forgetting my resolve.

"I see. You have yet to prove yourself to these ruffians, then?"

"Shut up," I said. "We shouldn't be talking."

"You're right. This hostage idea is crumbling down around my ears—not one of my prouder moments. Something tells me it's time to act."

The decisive words had scarcely left his mouth when he shoved me roughly aside and charged forward, dragging his sword from its scabbard as he ran. He had no sooner dived ahead than a green arrow whistled past the spot where his head had been only seconds before. The shaft, angled downward, nearly skimmed my shoulder as I tumbled to the ground from the force of the priest's shove. As I rolled back to my feet, I scanned the treetops and was rewarded with a quick glimpse of Kipp shimmied out on a low-hanging limb, bow in hand. I turned my attention back to the melee before me.

And a battle it was, though it shouldn't have been. A lone man clad in cumbersome priest's robes ought to have been no match for a handful of hardened brigands. But he was. None of the outlaws had anything better than hunting knives and daggers and they were unprepared to fend off the attack of a broadsword. The first outlaw to encounter the priest was swiftly cut down, not to stir again. A second outlaw danced in to deal a tap of his pike at the priest's chest and was quickly slashed across the forearm for it. I didn't see what else became of him.

I slipped my knives from their wrist sheaths and rushed to join my comrades, who were fanning out to form a ring around our sturdy opponent. As we closed in on him, the priest spun, managing to be everywhere at once. Brig had no sooner swung a powerful blow of his stave at the priest's head, when the broadsword was there to stop it. With a single slash, Brig's stave became two short sticks. I chose that moment of distraction to duck into the fray and jab at our enemy with one of my knives, but he avoided that too, with a long sidestep and a ringing slap across my shoulders with the flat of his blade.

Seething and feeling mocked, I was pushed

out of the fight by Brig, who positioned himself in front of me. I watched, helpless, as our opponent plunged his blade into Dannon's belly and spun to lop off Ladley's right arm, followed by his head, in two clean sweeps. The priest sustained no injuries, appearing hardly winded, and I began to believe he might finish us all.

The outlaws were clearly daunted by his skill. They stepped up their attack and the priest became a grey blur as he spun, slashed, and blocked. Never had I seen a man fight as he did. He moved with such speed I couldn't have targeted him even had I a bow and been competent at using it. His robes swirled outward, revealing the glint of chain mail underneath, and his eyes sparked with a fire like none I had ever witnessed. He seemed unstoppable as he slashed our disintegrating line to bits.

There were only three outlaws standing now, Brig, Kinsley, and I. The others were either dead or grounded with injuries. I suspected several feigned worse wounds than they possessed to avoid further combat with the formidable priest and I didn't blame them. It was unnerving being one of the few still in his path and I felt an urge, myself, to sit out this fight.

Instead, I straightened my back and kept a ready stance, trying to appear braver than I felt. I gripped the knives in my hands so tightly my knuckles ached. Brig hadn't given me permission to reenter the fray, but I didn't think I could afford not to. There was a brief pause of indecision and then Brig charged. He had collected what was left of his broken staff and he swung this at the priest's head, while Kinsley simultaneously attacked with a dagger.

The priest raised an arm and Brig's cudgel glanced off his elbow with an audible crack. Our opponent's injury must have been screaming painfully, but still he lashed out, his sword licking a shallow cut across Kinsley's arm. Then I watched, horrified, as his blade darted for Brig. Every thought flew from my mind except the need to defend the outlaw.

I ducked beneath the oncoming blade and threw myself into our enemy's ankles.

CHAPTER TEN

I T WASN'T A BRAVE TACTIC or well planned, but it worked. The priest rocked on his legs, I tightened my arms around his boots so he couldn't steady himself, and he fell backward, slamming into the ground. Immediately, I heard the quick crunch of approaching footsteps signaling Brig and Kinsley moving in and I gripped my arms more firmly around our opponent's legs.

I heard his hand scrabbling in the dirt for his dropped blade as he grated at me, "Release me or I'll be forced to kill you!"

I ignored his words and held fast.

"Wicked little wretch..." he muttered.

I wasn't in a position to see anything besides his dusty feet, but I heard the sound of his hand discovering his sword hilt. I braced myself for the blow I was certain would be forthcoming. It fell, ringing across my skull like hammer on anvil, and I saw bright lights. Stunned, I briefly lost awareness of my surroundings before consciousness came roaring back. I heard sounds of conflict around me and realized the priest had slipped out of my grasp.

Crawling dizzily to my knees, head ringing so

harshly I was powerless to do more once I got there than sit in the dirt, I observed the scene unfolding before me. The outlaws stood before the priest, obviously only going through the motions of a fight they didn't believe they could win. Kinsley's sleeve was soaked in red, his arm hanging limp. Brig stood weaponless, as if he would clash with the swordsman bare handed. His face spelled defeat and my throat constricted with fear as the priest drew back his blade.

"Wait!" The unexpected shout came from Kinsley. "There's no sense to this," he said to the priest. "You kill us and our lad in the tree up there will still shoot you afterward. It'll be a short-lived victory for you."

He indicated Kipp, crouched high in his tree.

The priest said, "Your boy would have to shoot me before I reached him and as he has yet to do so, I suspect he lacks either the skill or the nerve. I'll take my chances."

Only the way he panted between words gave away his weariness.

Kinsley said, "Kill him, kill all of us, and you only seal your fate. The captain of our band is a vengeful man with a deadly reputation. Maybe you've heard of him. Rideon the Red Hand."

He paused expectantly, but if he thought to find our enemy impressed, he must have been disappointed, for the priest's expression never altered. Kinsley frowned and continued with, "Rideon won't let you walk free to boast of besting his men for long. You might go on for a year or two thinking yourself safe, but the Hand has a long memory and a far reach. Sooner or later, the morning will come when you wake to find your throat slit and your family drowning in their blood."

The priest appeared unconcerned. "I have no family to fear for and, as you've already discovered for yourselves, my throat is singularly hard to slit," he said. "I think you attribute more power to this outlaw captain of yours than such a man could possibly possess. Still, you've captured my interest. Who is this 'Red Hand' people in these parts speak of with such dread?"

"I offer you the chance to find out," Kinsley said. "He'd like to meet a man with your skills."

"An interesting offer," said the priest. "But despite a degree of morbid curiosity, I've no desire to sit down opposite some murderous scoundrel as if we were on peaceable terms. It is not my habit to keep company with thieves and criminals."

Kinsley wasn't to be defeated. "A bargain, then? Allow us to keep our lives today and we'll return the favor the next time you pass through our woods."

"Now that is the sort of agreement I can appreciate," said the priest. "But let us go a step further, shall we? You allow these good traveling companions of mine to depart in peace and in full possession of all they bear with them and in exchange, I'll give you your lives."

Kinsley looked at once relieved and uncertain.

"The Hand will be angry if we return empty handed. It's not only about the goods. We were told a certain nobleman travels in your caravan under the guise of a commoner. Rideon believes such a person would bring in a tidy ransom."

"I have been in the company of these folk since Black Cliffs. I can assure you none of them are any person of importance, traveling under pretense. Each is as humble as he appears. As an Honored One, you know my word is beyond question."

Kinsley hesitated, but even he knew priests didn't lie. "Very well, I'll tell the Hand you've sworn it for truth," the outlaw said. "You and your companions are free to go as you please."

There was no gripping of hands to seal the agreement. The priest simply turned his back on us and began helping the travelers reload their belongings. Many of them had already taken the opportunity to flee off down the road and those who remained gathered their scattered possessions with a haste that said they were just glad to be leaving with their lives. I believed they would have abandoned their belongings right there on the road if not for the priest's organization. I half expected some of the outlaws to break the truce and attack the priest as soon as he was off his guard, but they didn't. Kinsley, Brig, and a handful of others who conveniently found themselves able to stand again busied themselves with checking our injured.

Brig came over to inspect my head injury and not until I felt his hands trembling as they fingered the lump where the priest's sword hilt had struck me did I realize how anxious he'd been for me. Awkward at his concern, I assured him I was well enough, although my head continued to throb so that I wasn't entirely sure of the truth to my words. Brig glared daggers at the priest's back but made no irrational move toward him and I was thankful for that, as I didn't feel up to defending him just now.

He ordered me not to walk about until I regained my color, so I sat and concentrated on nothing but slowing the waves of dizziness pulsing over me. I was so distracted that I didn't immediately notice when **someone** sank to the ground beside me.

"Mind if I join you for a moment to catch my breath?" asked the priest, as casually as if we had not been trying to kill one another mere moments before.

I eyed him warily. "Won't your friends leave without you? They seem in a rush to be on their way."

"I can catch up," he said carelessly.

Out of the corner of one eye, I watched as he rested his sword across his knee and dragged a grey sleeve across his sweaty face. This was my first chance to study the man as more than a blur of motion and without the distraction of keeping out of his sword's reach. He looked weary, covered in dust and spattered with the blood of my comrades. Beneath the grime was a strong, broad face with a long jaw and a nose as straight as it was wide. I was unsurprised no previous combatants had ever been able to get past his wide sweep to mar the clean proportions of his face.

Unable to resist my curiosity, I probed at the man's mind with a thin thread of magic. I didn't know him well enough to form a good connection, but for just a moment I brushed against his consciousness. And then I lost the link as he started, whirling to seize me roughly by the jaw and glare piercingly into my eyes. Startled as much by the knowing in his expression as by the abrupt action, I jerked the tendril of magic into myself again. Or tried to. But suddenly, it was being wrested from my grip and flung back at me with shocking force. The jar to my senses was almost a physical one and I gasped as if a heavy weight had slammed into me.

"Serves you right for prying where you don't belong," said the priest, putting a steadying hand on my shoulder, despite the harsh words. "Hold on a moment and take deep breaths until the weakness passes. Perhaps I was rougher than I intended to be."

"I don't understand. What did you do to me?" I asked. "I've never felt anything like that."

"You intruded where you had no right. I scooped you up and threw you back into yourself," he said. "Until you think you're strong enough to out-magic me, keep your grubby little mind out of my head."

"My mind isn't grubby," I said. "And I couldn't

be less interested in what goes on in yours."

"If you say so."

He turned his shoulder to me and appeared content to forget my presence. But his words were sinking in and, looking at him askance, I realized that for the first time in years I was in the presence of another magicker. I couldn't let the opportunity pass. Not when I had so many questions. But did I trust this peculiar stranger enough to ask them?

As I debated within myself, I saw the priest's lips quirk upward in a faint smile.

"You're reading my thoughts," I accused. "Surely what you said about intruding on other people's minds goes both ways, my lord."

He looked startled. "Why do you call me that?"

"You're not the only one who knows things," I said smugly. "You told Kinsley that none of your companions was a nobleman traveling in disguise, but you said nothing of yourself. You see, I'm accustomed to the cunning ways dishonest priests can twist their words. There are a thousand ways to lie without uttering an untruth. But then, I suppose you aren't a real Honored anyway, are you? Everyone knows priests of the Light take a vow against violence. Who ever heard of one carrying a blade and not hesitating to use it?"

He smiled. "I assure you, my young friend, the priest in me is every bit as real as the warrior, and the nobleman's blood is just another piece of the whole. I gave up my title and inheritance long ago to become one of the Blades of Justice. It's the only priestly order permitting violence—but always for a righteous cause. I've now retired from that life as well and these days I travel through the land on nothing more urgent than my whims."

He glanced around and lowered his voice. "I hope I can trust you to keep the secret of my identity to yourself. I don't think either of us wants to stir up more trouble with your comrades."

I had questions, not the least of which was why he would give up a comfortable inheritance to join an order of warrior priests.

But he evaded further questions by saying, "As for your other accusation, I was not prying into your thoughts. You were throwing them at me. You must train yourself to keep your feelings guarded in the presence of those with the talent for sensing them. It's not good, walking around, crying out your thoughts and emotions to everyone within hearing distance."

I shrugged. "I can't prevent myself thinking. The mind runs free as it pleases, whether given permission or not."

He said, "There's a discipline I could teach you, if you like. Someone should. I cannot imagine how your parents neglected such basic instruction."

"My parents are dead," I said stiffly. "Killed in the Praetor's cleansings."

"I'm sorry to hear it," he said. "The province lost many magickers during those years, but the worst of those times are over now. And the thinning of our numbers only makes it all the more imperative those of us remaining teach our younglings what they need to know to survive with their abilities."

"My magic and I have gotten along just fine up to now," I said. "Anyway, assuming I needed help, you're scarcely the tutor I would choose for myself."

"We can't always be particular about what we learn or where. You may never receive such an offer again and I know that would disappoint you. I can feel the thirst for knowledge burning within you. You're just waiting to be talked into it."

"You're reading my mind again," I said, drawing back.

"Your thoughts are not words to be read off a page," he corrected. "Following emotions is a subtle thing, like catching a whisper or a scent carried on the breeze. You don't need to see the source to be aware of the resulting effect. Anyway, think on my offer. There is much I could teach you, given a few months, if you chose to come with me."

"That's impossible. My entire life is in Dimmingwood. I could no more leave my friends or the forest than I could abandon a part of myself. It's not that I don't want to..."

"I know. But what you want more is to be him," he said.

"Him? Him who?"

"This Red Hand everybody speaks of."

I wasn't sure how to respond to that, but he gave me no opportunity to do so.

"Never mind," he said. "If you should reconsider, you can find me at the Temple of Light in Selbius on the first day of Middlefest. If you miss me there, inquire among the river people for Hadrian. I am known to them."

He left me with much to think over. Our bedraggled band returned to Red Rock, empty-handed but for the dead and injured we carried with us. At first, Rideon and the rest of the band were disinclined to believe we had suffered such damage at the hands of a lone swordsman dressed in priest's robes. But no one could deny the proof of the corpses we buried that day. Another wounded man died before the day was out.

These losses only furthered my confusion. I didn't know what to make of Hadrian's offer. The knowledge he promised filled me with a frightening excitement, even as I wondered if it would be traitorous to seek out the company of a man who had slaughtered my fellows. I trailed Javen the rest of the day, helping him care for the wounded, but my mind was scarcely on the task.

As I worked, I heard a lot of talk about the gray-clad priest, some of it angry, some reluctantly admiring. All the while I bathed bloody cuts and held slashed sections of skin together for Javen to stitch up, I kept thinking of new questions to ask Hadrian if we met again.

CHAPTER ELEVEN

D URING THE FOLLOWING WEEKS, TRAVELERS and traders flocked to Selbius from the surrounding countryside, intent on arriving early before the Middlefest celebrations. Those who passed through Dimming left the shadowed wood significantly poorer than they had entered it.

There was a constant flow of comings and goings about both our camps during that time. To my disappointment, I was largely left out of the activity. Brig's fears, seemingly confirmed by my mishap with the priest, had again become a deterrent. I was also kept busy with the menial tasks around camp the others no longer had time for. That I couldn't blame on Brig, although I was certain if there was a way he could have increased my workload to keep me at Red Rock more, he would have.

These were my thoughts one afternoon in mid-spring, as I stalked through the cool forest shadows with Terrac. I led us here in hopes of hunting down one of the sly hedge rabbits that loved to nibble among the thickets of hopeberries.

Our band had feasted on thin potato porridge for three consecutive days, and I meant to have meat for supper tonight of it took me all day to hunt it down.

Terrac, unfortunately, didn't share my determination. He crashed carelessly through the bushes, heedless of the noise he made, as he collected bright berries to be later mashed into inks for his scribbling. Whatever game was in the area was probably fleeing his noise even now, but I stifled my rising irritation. No point in taking my frustrations out on him.

"I don't think there's any game here, Terrac," I said. "I'm going to try over near Dancing Creek, all right? Maybe you should wait for me here. Just keep on with what you're doing."

In place of response, Terrac gave a startled cry. He had moved on ahead of me and a high wall of brambles concealed him from my view.

"Terrac? What is it?" I asked.

No answer.

I moved after him, concerned he might have stepped on a venomous snake or happened upon an angry bear. Dragging my hunting knife free of my belt in case I was called on to defend us, I charged into the bramble bush, ignoring the sharp thorns snagging at my skin and clothes, as I wrestled my way through to Terrac.

He was on his knees bent over the form of an unconscious man, lying in a shallow pool of blood. The stranger lay with his belly to the earth, the toes of his boots pushed into the dirt, his hands formed into claws, gripping tightly at a clump of weeds as though he had tried to drag himself further, before surrendering to his weakness. I dropped to one knee at his side and together Terrac and I turned him over.

His face was so battered and covered in blood that it took me a moment to note the distinctive scar lining his brow to the hairline and a narrow shock of white hair growing in that spot. It was this which helped me identify him as Garad from Molehill, one of our men. I didn't know him well, for he hadn't been up to Red Rock much, but I vaguely remembered him as a quiet man who used to chat with Brig.

"He lives," Terrac told me, quietly.

Pressing my ear over the man's heart, I listened to the faint uneven rhythm. As we watched, his eyelids suddenly flew open and he glared around him wildly.

"Garad, it's all right." I hastened to soothe him. "We're no enemies. You know us."

He fastened his gaze on me and I thought there was confused recognition in his eyes before a convulsion of pain distorted his features.

Unthinkingly, I summoned my magic and directed it toward the suffering man, attempting to convey a sense of calm or comfort to his mind. Friends were here. There was no fear, no pain. I knew it was hopeless the moment I touched him. I could feel his life flickering like a guttering candle between existence and oblivion, and I didn't think my calming suggestions were reaching him. He was too deeply steeped in his suffering. Still, I felt his reason fighting determinedly to the forefront.

He drew a ragged breath and I expected him to scream out his pain, but he didn't. Somehow he held the torment back enough to grate out his message. "Fists... t-tell the Hand it was Resid and the Fists. T-tried to fight back, but they knew we were coming. Warn... the others..."

I left Terrac to memorize the message because I could listen with only half my mind. Most of my attention focused on the inward struggle to find and unravel the threads of Garad's pain and it wasn't working. His emotions were tangled and confused, and I couldn't insinuate my thoughts into them. I tried another tactic, tracing the pain to its source and wrapping my mind around it. I couldn't smother the force, but I could hold the worst of it back from his consciousness.

It was then the pain slammed into me. I was stunned as I took its strength into myself. Consumed by the agony that was now mine, I toppled backward to the ground. I gritted my teeth and arched my back.

"Ilan! Ilan, what is it?" I heard Terrac shout, but his voice filtered to me from a great distance and I couldn't concentrate enough to form an answer. There was too much pain to leave space for anything else.

"Get help!" I grated.

Terrac looked desperate. "I can't! I don't know my way back to camp without you!"

I was scarcely aware of his words because I was blacking out. The instant my consciousness began to slip, I lost my hold on the pain. The agony flowed from me as if a dam had burst and reverted to its natural course, pouring back into the prone figure beside me. Garad cried out as it coursed through his body again, but selfish relief washed over me. I was terribly weakened and I sucked in air as if I couldn't get enough of it, every fiber of me acutely aware of how wonderful it was to be free of the pain.

I grasped Tearrac's wrist to stop his hopeless yelling for help. "Be quiet and help me up," I said wearily.

He looked confused. "You're all right now? But what happened to you?"

"Never mind, I'll explain later. Just help me sit up."

He assisted me and in a moment I was sitting upright. Beside us, the injured outlaw screamed again. I had no time to collect my strength as, staggered by weakness, I drew myself to my feet.

"What are you doing?" Terrac asked, steadying me.

"One of us has to fetch help. You don't know the way, so that leaves me."

"Do you think you can get there without collapsing?"

"Of course," I lied. "I have no choice."

"Then bring Javen. And Rideon. This man's just holding on long enough to get his message to the Hand."

"I'll be quick," I promised. I'd run myself to death if I had to.

Dredging up what energy I could, I pushed my way back toward Red Rock as speedily as my weak legs would carry me. Terrac, I quickly realized, could have run circles around me just now. But of course, his circles wouldn't have been in the right direction.

I dragged myself onward until I reached camp. There, I discovered Javen wasn't to be found and I could waste no time looking for him. As soon as I could gather breath, I explained the situation to a handful of the outlaws. Someone hunted down Rideon and we left the camp with a dozen or so of the band following my lead.

Garad was dead when we arrived. Terrac had drawn his eyes closed, but it did little to lend him an appearance of peace. His face was distorted in a snarl of agony, his mouth open in a frozen cry, and I felt a selfish sense of relief I had been too far away to witness the end.

Rideon dropped to a knee at the dead man's side, asking Terrac, "Did he say anything more of what befell him?"

Expression drawn, Terrac glanced toward me and said, "His pain was too great to say much. He ranted through his screams, but I couldn't make sense of most of it. He and several others were on an errand near Tinker's Path when they were attacked, ambushed by a troop of Fists who knew enough to be sure where to lie in wait. An outlaw of yours, one called Resid, betrayed them. There were no other survivors."

"I know that location," one of our men spoke up. "Heard some of them earlier planning a trip to the traveler's way huts. If you pop in there quick enough, you can scrounge around for supplies the travelers have left behind for the next folk what stops by."

"Why did I never hear of these intentions?" Rideon demanded.

The outlaw scratched his shaggy beard. "I, uh, couldn't say, Hand. I didn't think it was nothing worth mentioning and I guess the others didn't either. Anyway, I wasn't in on the discussion myself. All I know is Mabias, Brig, and Spearneck were going, together with a handful of others. I guess Garad and Resid from Molehill were among them."

My stomach lurched at the mention of Brig. Surely he was mistaken—Brig couldn't have been among those slaughtered. The possibility was too shattering too accept. I struggled after a shred of hope, anything to hold onto. None escaped, according to Garad, I reminded myself, but hadn't Garad been in such pain that even Terrac admitted half his words were senseless rantings? One other might still have survived—*must* have survived—I decided desperately. Brig was not a man to die easily.

Rideon carried on with his thoughts, apparently unconcerned with the fates of his men. "Resid," he mused, "was a new member. What does he know? Everything?"

Kinsley stepped nearer. "He's scarcely left Molehill, Hand. Never been to Red Rock and shouldn't even know where it is. I keep the new ones in the dark until they've proven themselves trustworthy. The other men know that's my rule and are usually pretty close-mouthed around new recruits."

"All except a select few who invited him into their secret plans," Rideon snapped. "How many others has he wheedled confidences from, sidling his way into their trust until they volunteered more information than they should?"

Kinsley said, "This is my fault for failing to search the new members carefully enough. I let a spy slip in among us."

"You did," Rideon agreed. "But there'll be time for whining about your carelessness later. We've more immediate problems to hand. We've got to evacuate Molehill if it isn't too late. Red Rock, too. I'll take no chances on what Resid may or may not have discovered. We have to operate under the assumption the Fists and their spy now know as much about us as we do ourselves. There's no saying how much time we have, so we must act quickly."

He spun on Terrac. "When did this ambush occur?"

Terrac shrugged. "Garad didn't say, but I imagine it must have taken a man in his condition a while to cover so much distance."

Rideon said, "Then let us waste no time. It appears we have little enough of it. Kinsley and the rest of you, come with me. Except you, Cadon. I want you to run up to Molehill as quickly as you can run. Spread the word to evacuate to the part of the forest where the trees don't green. We'll meet up and form our plans there."

I interrupted with the question no one else seemed concerned about. "But what of our missing men? What of Brig?"

Rideon continued giving out instructions as if I hadn't spoken. Only Terrac looked at me with sympathy. "I think it's too late for them, Ilan," he said. "I'm sorry."

"Don't be," I said firmly. "Brig lives." I refused to consider the alternative.

Terrac frowned. "Garad was dying. It's unlikely he would have dared lie to a priest, even if he had some unfathomable cause to."

I scarcely heard him. I was thinking that if I never saw Brig again, I'd never have the chance to mend our damaged friendship. All I wanted was a chance to explain myself to him, to return things to the way they once were between us. Suddenly, every sly act of disrespect, every insult I'd ever tossed at him, was a bitter memory to me, like a blade twisted deep in my gut. It would haunt me forever if I didn't get the chance to take it all back.

Rideon had finished issuing orders and the others were dispersing to carry out his commands when I intercepted him, seizing the front of his jerkin and thrusting my face into his.

I said, "What are you going to do for Brig and the rest? You cannot mean to leave them to their fates."

My captain looked down on me coldly. "Didn't you hear the priest boy say they were dead? They're beyond our aid. Now out of my way, hound. There's important work to be carried out and little time in which to accomplish it."

"But maybe they weren't all killed. We have only Garad's word on that! I won't believe anything could have happened to Brig until I've seen it with my own eyes."

Rideon shook me off impatiently. "Then you're doomed to a lifetime of wondering. We've more immediate problems to occupy ourselves with than worrying about what happened to Brig. Like getting all our people out of Red Rock and Molehill before they meet the same fate as Garad here. Now, I know what you're thinking, but I forbid you or anyone else to go running off after a corpse. We've the living to defend, so let's move on and do what we can for those who aren't beyond saving."

I wouldn't listen. "I'm telling you, I can bring Brig back. I can and I will!"

"And where do you expect to find him?" Rideon asked. "Do you think the Praetor's men just leave the bodies of outlaws lying out on the roads for carrion? Do you never pay attention to anything that happens around you? No, the Fists bring their victims, alive or dead, to Selbius, where the crowds may witness the Praetor's justice. Brig's remains will be displayed on the city walls or hung up in the market square, alongside the rotting bones of anyone else who has ever dared to flout the Praetor's rule."

I stood stupidly, factoring this new information into my plans as he shoved past. I was scarcely aware of his leaving. What he said changed nothing. I needed to see for myself whether Brig was truly dead. And even if he were... I couldn't allow his corpse to be dishonored in the way Rideon described. One way or another, I must save him, and next to this, Rideon's orders meant little.

I said, "Terrac, how far to Selbius from the way huts on Tinker's Path?"

Terrac must have been following my thinking, for he looked uneasy. "You know these woods better than I do."

I said, "I think it's about a half day, as the raven flies, but it'll take longer for them." There was no question as to who 'they' were. "They'll follow the road and that'll cost them time. There'd be no taking their horses straight through Heeflin's Bog. And if I know Brig and the rest, I suspect the Fists will also have injured men of their own, which will slow them down further. But they've a good headstart on us so we've no time to waste. Come on, I'll need your help."

"No."

The priest boy's refusal drew me to a halt before I had gone three steps. I wasn't much surprised by his response and had my argument prepared.

"Brig saved your life when you came here, nursed you back to health as much as I did," I reminded him. "You can leave him to his fate now? Is that the kind of honor your old priests taught you?"

Terrac shook his head. "I know what you have in mind, Ilan. But there's only the two of us against an unknown number of them. As a man of the robe, I cannot fight, even to save my life, so I'd be useless to you. I'm sorry for you and for Brig, truly, but Rideon has given his orders and for once I am in agreement with him."

I was furious but could waste no more time attempting to argue him out of his cowardice. "I see. Well then, may your friends ever be as faithful to you."

I turned my back on him and set off into the underbrush without another look. I sensed I had shamed him and he was undergoing some internal struggle, so it was no surprise when, after a short pause, he came running after me.

We kept silent as we strode together through the thick trees. I set a brisk pace and neither of us could afford to waste breath speaking. Every instinct within me screamed at me to run, to hasten to Brig's side as quickly as my legs could speed me, but I restrained myself. We had a long distance to cover and there was no sense in spending all our strength this early.

CHAPTER TWELVE

IT WAS MID-AFTERNOON WHEN WE came upon the traveler's way huts along the Tinker Path. It was easy to see the evidence of what happened in this place. The ground around the buildings was blood-soaked and churned with the prints of men and horses alike. There must have been a dozen or more Fists here, but I didn't share that fact with Terrac. His resolve was weak enough.

Behind the way huts we found our men, or what was left of them. I saw Mabias, Spearneck, and a couple others I didn't know as well. The Fists hadn't troubled themselves with carrying the whole remains back to Selbius, but every corpse had been beheaded, the decapitated bodies left where they fell. I identified the dead mostly by clothing or distinctive markings on their bodies. Of the traitor, Resid, there was no sign and I could only assume he had ridden away with the Fists.

Resid was not the only man missing. My heart climbed back out of my throat as I realized Brig was not among the dead. I searched the sheds and the surrounding area, thinking he might have crawled, injured, a short distance, but all I found was his bone-handled hunting knife lying behind one of the sheds. My search here done, I slipped the knife into my belt and hurried a protesting Terrac off the road.

Much as I regretted the necessity, we had to leave the rest of our men where they lay. There wasn't time to deal with any kind of burial. I still had no way of knowing whether it was a live prisoner or a cold corpse I was chasing after, but as long as there was any hope for Brig, I couldn't give up. We pushed on through the wood, making for the shortcut through Heeflin's Bog. I had to catch the Fists before Selbius. Once Brig was within the city walls there would be little chance of getting him back.

We were weary and wet to the waist from our trudge through the bog when we came again onto the path the Fists took to Selbius. I was as dejected as I was exhausted, for I knew too much time had been wasted in the crossing of the marsh, and I feared we couldn't hope to catch our quarry, let alone cut them off before they reached this point. But I wouldn't admit this to Terrac, nor would I give in to his continual requests to turn back. We pushed on, following in the tracks of the company that had already passed this way.

It was past sundown when we approached a cluster of buildings looming ahead, out of the darkness. We were still within Dimming's borders, but only just, and I recognized the ramshackle buildings set a little aside from the road as one of the abandoned woods folk farms. Thunder rumbled overhead and a few cold sprinkles began to fall as the holding came into view.

The last of the Fist's tracks were being washed from the road but not before I saw their horses had turned off the way, veering into the direction of the abandoned hold buildings. I caught the dim glow of light filtering out the shuttered windows of the hold house and felt a surge of hope. If the Fists had stopped here to take shelter from the storm...

Terrac was less pleased than I to have caught up to our enemies, but I wouldn't hear his warnings. I struck off for the hold buildings and he reluctantly followed. I shushed his protests as we neared and we made several careful, silent circuits around the property, wary of sentries. When I was satisfied our enemies were oblivious to our approach, we crept closer. The rain and the dark were our allies, shielding us from unfriendly eyes.

We moved in as near as we dared, then dropped to our bellies in a little stand of weeds on a gentle rise overlooking the hold house. My heart was beating fast and I expected discovery at any moment. Terrac parted the grasses and peered ahead. Seconds passed before I felt him stiffen beside me.

He said, "There's a man circling the outer sheds. He doesn't stop to look around, just keeps his head down and moves with purpose. Nothing else stirs."

"Is he one of the Praetor's men?" I whispered.

"Now how can I know that?"

I craned my neck, but Terrac was slightly ahead of me and I couldn't see past him without the commotion of rearranging myself.

I said, "Does he look like a fighting man? Is he armed? Outfitted in the Praetor's colors? A Fist would have a bear's head worked into his breastplate."

"At this distance do you think I can see a breastplate, let alone a bear's head on it? It's too dark even to make out his colors. Besides, he's gone now, disappeared into the barn."

I sighed and risked repositioning myself for a clearer view. My movements made the tall grass rustle and I hoped no one was near enough to notice. I now had a good look at the hold house and its dilapidated outbuildings. I could see no movement below. No men, no sign of horses. The only evidence anyone was down there at all was Terrac's claim to have seen someone—that and the spill of light issuing from the open doorway and windows.

I located the barn, an old leaning structure beyond the house. I waited and was at length rewarded when a lone figure wandered out its doors. I couldn't make out any particulars about him. I followed his progress as he ducked his head against the falling rain and hastened to the dry shelter of the hold house. Not a sentry, then, just a man checking on his horse. For a moment he was outlined in the doorway as he stepped into the house and I caught the glint of light falling across the steel at his hip and a quick glimpse of black leather over scarlet.

"A Praetor's man, all right," I whispered to Terrac. "There must be more of them inside the house or in the outbuildings."

A plan began to take shape in my head as I scanned the shadowy rooftops.

"And how are we to discover whether Brig is with them?" Terrac asked.

I pushed aside my qualms. I would do whatever I must to get Brig back, and if that meant using Terrac as unwitting bait, so be it.

I said, "I see no sign of a watch, meaning either they haven't set any or their sentries are too well hidden to be seen. The first, I think, for I've pretty good night vision and I can't make out anyone hiding in the shadows." I tried to sound confident because I didn't want him turning tail right when I had use for him. "But we won't risk everything on that supposition. We'll go down just as if there were lookouts."

Here was where I must slip in the crucial point and pray I could convince him of it. "You'll go first," I said. "One is less conspicuous than two. Slip down to the house and try to get close enough for a look in the windows. Don't come back until you can tell me how many Fists there are and if Brig is among them. I think it would be best if I wait here for you."

"Yes, I'm sure you do," Terrac said, frowning. "How is it I'm the one handling the dangerous part when this was your idea in the first place?"

How, indeed? I scrambled for a plausible excuse. "Because you're the quicker of us and have the best chance of slipping back and forth unseen."

His expression showed he wasn't buying that horse, so I struck out with a better lie. "And because I'm, um, afraid."

"Afraid?" The mingled surprise and disbelief in his voice made me wish I had thought of something better.

I hurried to elaborate. "I mean, I'm afraid for Brig. You know how close we were and you've seen what the Fists do to their enemies. I'm afraid of what we could find down there and of how I'll react. I might go mad and do something foolish to get us captured or killed."

I inwardly blessed his gullibility as I saw the disbelief fade from his face. He nodded and said, "I suppose there is sense in what you say. Maybe it would be for the best if I'm the one to go. I'll bring the news back to you, whether good or bad."

Suffering an unexpected stab of remorse, I caught his arm as he started to turn away. I opened my mouth to confess, but what came out instead was, "You're a good would-be priest, Terrac. An honest man. You can tell that to anyone."

I couldn't be sure if he detected the instruction behind my words, but he seemed to catch the seriousness of my tone. "I don't know how good I am, but I think any friend would do as much. Now I'd best do this thing quickly if I'm going to do it at all."

A part of me felt relief that he hadn't understood. "Yes, of course," I said. "Thank you, Terrac."

He gave my shoulder a reassuring squeeze and then he was away. I kept my head low, watching his awkward progress as he moved off. Slithering down the hillock on his stomach and scrambling to his feet at the bottom, he ran doubled over in the direction of the hold house in the clumsiest stealth approach I'd ever seen.

I returned my gaze to the sentry I had previously observed lurking beneath the shadowed eaves of the house. I could only hope he would take my friend in for questioning, rather than killing him on the spot, but there was little I could do to ensure that and my conscience smote me. Terrac was my friend and here I was betraying him for my own schemes. But when I thought of Brig, my guilt was instantly silenced. For me, Brig came ahead of any other and this was the only way I could think of keeping the Fists busy while I searched for him.

From here on out, speed was important. I slithered quickly through the grass until I made it down the brow of the hill and then kept low to the earth as I circled to the back of the hold yard. The looming shadow of the barn was my goal because if Brig was dead, I imagined the Fists would have stowed his corpse in just such a place. I had to cancel out that horrible possibility before I could lay any rescue plans. I reached the barn without being seen and kept to the shadows, creeping around to the front entrance. The door was rotten and protested softly when I tried it so that I hesitated to test it further.

Abruptly, a strangled cry rang out across the yard. Although I'd been expecting it, I started anyway. The shout was immediately followed by sounds of a struggle and I dropped flat to the ground, training my gaze on the house. I made out two dark silhouettes scuffling in the shadows. The smaller of the two was actually giving a fair account of himself, but inevitably, his larger opponent soon drew something from his belt, possibly a knife. I was too far away to be certain. He hooked his arm around Terrac from behind, pressed the object against the boy's throat and Terrac immediately stiffened and fell still. I held my breath, praying he would have the sense to heed the Fist's orders. Apparently he did, and I watched as he cooperatively allowed the knife man to drag him backwards toward the entrance of the house.

I wasn't the only one to hear the struggle. A handful of Fists came rushing to fill the open doorway of the house. Apparently caught sleeping, no one had taken the time to throw clothing on and they stood in various stages of undress, many of them barefoot, but all with swords in hand. A few stepped out to help their comrade with his captive, while others cast wary gazes out into the wet night, probably wondering whether they could expect more intruders to descend at any moment.

Everything was in Terrac's hands now. I could only hope whatever he told our enemies would dissuade them from searching the yard for his companions. I couldn't afford to linger any longer and used my enemies' brief distraction to try the barn door again. I winced at its muffled groan but didn't hesitate this time, slipping through the doorway and into the building. The blackness within was even deeper than that outside and I stood, disoriented, just inside the door. I allowed my eyes time to adjust to the dimness before beginning a swift search of the interior from top to bottom.

It was as I was giving up a hasty exploration of the hayloft that I made a peculiar discovery. My foot scuffed against something hidden beneath the thin layer of moldy straw on the floor and hurried though I was, instinct made me kneel to uncover the object. Certainly I had no time for distractions, but the thing had an odd shape and for a moment curiosity took over so that I quickly dusted aside the straw to pick it up. In the darkness it was difficult to discern what it was and I nearly cast it aside as a crooked bit of wood with a string tied to it. Then, recognizing its feel, I took a closer look and realized I was holding a bow.

CHAPTER THIRTEEN

T HIS SEEMS LIKE AN UNLIKELY *place to find such a weapon,* I thought, turning it around in my hands and noting how light and sturdy it felt. From the little I knew of bows, I judged this to be a good one. In the darkness, my fingers traced a line of carvings spiraling down the wooden arms. I'd never heard of anyone putting such detailed effort into the making of a bow, and I thought I would like to see it in better lighting.

I had no sooner had the thought, than the weapon warmed beneath my touch and glowed with a faint orangey light. What evil magic was this? Startled, I threw the weapon away from me and it sailed over the edge of the loft. After a moment's hesitation, I worked up the courage to clamber down the rope ladder after it and found it lying in a pile of straw.

When I dared to reach out and tentatively take the bow into my hands again, I was relieved to find it cold once more. The glow was gone too. Had I only imagined it before? Yes, that must be it. Impulsively, I slung the bow over my shoulder and returned to my search.

I made a hasty exploration of the rest of the interior, disturbing the Fist's horses as I went so that they began whickering loudly and shifting in their stalls. Fearful lest anyone come to investigate the noise, I abandoned the barn and moved on to the outbuildings. I crept from one building to the next, heart sinking as I failed to find Brig locked away in any of them. I told myself this was a hopeful sign. If he wasn't out here, he must be under guard in the house and that at least meant he was alive. What was happening inside the hold house now? What were they doing to Terrac and what was he telling them? I quickened my search.

The next shed I poked my head into was a privy and the one after that appeared to be a place for storing herbs. Dark shapes hung from the ceiling and it took me a moment to realize they were bunches of dried plants suspended upside down. The pungent scents of thickleaf and ravenspoison were heavy in the air. There was a low worktable scattered with cracked earthenware pottery and the rotting remnants of more clusters of weeds and leaves.

The shed held the bitter smell of decay and I lingered only long enough to determine Brig wasn't there. Backing out of the building, I pulled the door to and turning away, stumbled over something. A stick of wood? No, it was a man's outstretched arm. In the shadows I could barely make out his still form lying in a heap against the side of the shed. His shaven head was tilted at a side angle, his bearded face half buried in the dirt. Large crimson blotches darkened the back of his tunic. My stomach clenched and with a strangled cry I dropped to my knees and flipped the body over.

I knew Brig was dead even as I felt for a heartbeat. Always before, when he was near, I could sense the life burning within him. But now I felt nothing from him, not even the barest tendril of warmth. He had been dead a while, and mingled grief and fury coursed through me as I saw evidence of torture. Despite what I felt, I couldn't seem to shed tears. My throat hurt, but my eyes were drier than sand. I bent over him, gathering his still form in my arms as best I was able. He had always been a heavy man and in death, his body had grown rigid, resisting my efforts. I huddled over his form, cradling it protectively, as he had sheltered me when I was small. My teeth were clenched so hard my jaw ached and I welcomed the pain, wishing for more.

I sat there for an age, drowning in grief and anger and forgetting all sense of time or purpose. Eventually I became aware of the weight of my new bow slung across my back and strangely, this brought me back to myself. I remembered I had a task before me and my heart hardened with resolve. I remembered how Rideon said they would display Brig's remains as a gruesome spectacle in Selbius. I thought of the sons Brig rarely spoke of, probably young men by now, and wondered what was the likelihood they would ever visit the city, see their father strung up in that way, and know him? I thought of Netta, who had left him for his thieving ways and wondered whether she would be pleased or sorry to see him come to such an end. Whatever she felt, I knew Brig would have hated her to see him so.

I shook the thought from my mind. If I wanted to spare my old friend that fate, I needed to keep my head clear. It was past time I took all of us away from this place, Terrac, too, if I could manage it. The plan I formed was not a clear one and certainly not brilliant, but it was all that came to me just then. I had no time to dwell on the particulars or the many possible failings.

I forced myself to abandon Brig's lifeless body and ducked back into the herb shed where I collected all the crushed ravenspoison I could find. It was dark and I had to identify the vials of dried herbs by smell, rather than sight. I mentally thanked Javen for teaching me all he knew of herbal concoctions and remedies. I worked quickly, stuffing my pockets full of vials, mindful my presence could be discovered at any moment. Then I hurried back to the barn, moving stealthily along the edges of the yard. I managed not to attract the attention of the sentries if there were still any around and slipped back into the relative safety of the shadowed building, where I emptied the vials entirely into the drinking water of the Fist's horses. I spared only one mount, a strong looking gray I had need of.

I also found the Fists' waterskins hung up alongside the riding gear, and I tipped a little herbal powder into these as well. I had no real expectation of anyone drinking enough to do them harm, since the taste should quickly warn the drinker against further sampling. Still, I thought it worth a try. Several of the horses were dipping their noses into their water buckets even as I left. I felt bad about the animals but reminded myself ravenspoison wasn't fatal, only sickening enough to put a man—or a horse—off his feet for a day or two.

Outside, I found a battered old onion cart. Its sides were rotten, but the bed and wheels might be sturdy enough for my purpose. I slipped back into the barn for horse and harness, which I brought out by way of a narrow back door I discovered in my earlier search. Even with the use of this concealed exit, I couldn't imagine how my movements had thus far failed to capture my enemies' attention. I could only be grateful for whatever Terrac was doing in there to keep them occupied. If only he could buy me a few more minutes... I longed for something to happen, anything, to keep all eyes away from me a little longer.

A shout went up in the distance. "Fire!"

That would do. I didn't have time to wonder who raised the cry or what sparked it. I could only be grateful for the sudden commotion that erupted, as other shouts joined the first, followed by the echoing bang of the farmhouse door being flung open and the thundering of many feet pounding outdoors.

I led the horse forward and the rickety cart followed, wheels creaking and wobbling as if it would collapse into pieces at any moment. We kept to the outer ring of the holding, immersing ourselves among the deepest shadows. I could see the hold house now, one wall burning and greedy tongues of flame licking up to the wood-shingled roof. Fists poured out windows and doorways, scrambling to removed themselves and their gear from the path of the flames. The lightly falling rain did little to dampen the blaze and the winds of the storm spread the flames all the swifter.

A new shout rose up in the distance. "This is the boy's work! Find him and bring him back!"

No one paid heed to the order.

I almost smiled to myself. It appeared Terrac was a little cleverer than I'd thought him. I only hoped he had the sense to put this place behind him. When I reached the shed, I left my cart in the shadows. Stooping over Brig's motionless form, I took hold of his shoulders and attempted to lift him from the ground. He was heavier than I expected and I grunted with the effort. I realized my back suddenly felt strangely warm. Was that the bow again, radiating heat through my tunic? I hesitated in confusion.

The sound of a footfall behind me was all the warning I had. I dropped my burden and leapt to one side, dodging none too soon as a thick cudgel descended where my head had been mere seconds before. Rolling to my feet, I slid my knives from their wrist sheaths... and became vividly aware of a powerful stirring at the back of my consciousness. An unfamiliar, inner voice seemed to be hissing instructions at me, only I couldn't make out the words. Startled, I nearly froze in my confusion, but hesitating at this moment would mean death. I shoved the distracting voice aside and dove for my attacker with the single thought of silencing him before he alerted others. He clearly hadn't anticipated I would choose to attack him directly and I could have caught him with a blade squarely in the chest then. But I stayed my hand at the last possible second. This enemy had a familiar face. Not a foe, but one of ours. Resid.

I hesitated and the outlaw seized the opportunity to launch another blow at my midsection. He hadn't got his full strength behind it, but when his cudgel connected with my ribs, the force still knocked the breath from me and sent me reeling backward to slam into the wall of the shed behind me. Pain raged like fire up my injured side as my adversary lifted his club for another swing, this one aimed at my head. Again, the whispered commands hissed through my mind and I could almost make them out this time. I dodged Resid's swing, feeling the wind from it whistle past my ear, and staggered sideways, the pain in my ribs slowing my movements. I tripped over Brig's sprawled form and reeled backward, attempting to keep my legs under me, knowing if I allowed myself to meet the ground, the fight was over. I would be finished as surely as Brig was. Brig, who had been sold out by a comrade, a man he believed he could trust.

The angry thought sent a surge of strength through me. I regained my balance and lashed out with one booted foot, catching Resid in the belly. My enemy doubled over and I dodged in to swipe my twin knives at him. I aimed for his throat, but he turned his head at the last instant and I dealt him, instead, a shallow slash across one cheek and a deeper stroke into the side of the neck, inadvertently finding an artery. A dark fountain of blood spewed outward.

An approving murmur seemed to come from somewhere in my head. Was it my magic speaking to me? That had never happened before, but I had no time to puzzle over it. Resid, stunned and weakened, stumbled toward me still. He moved awkwardly and I had no difficulty ducking beneath his next onslaught and slashing across the wrist with which he held his cudgel. The weapon fell from his fingers and I moved easily in to open his throat with my blades. My enemy collapsed at my feet and I felt no pity. He should never have turned on Rideon. Or at least, he should not have killed Brig in the bargain.

Looking down on Brig, a wave of misery washed over me and in this sudden bleakness, my original plan felt useless. But I had gone too far to turn back now. I pushed aside my weariness and the throbbing pain in my ribs and knelt again to haul at Brig's shoulders. I wasn't sure if it was the exhaustion or the burning in my side, but the dead man now felt like a load of bricks, and for all my efforts, I couldn't have dragged him to the cart if the simple act could have restored his life. Giving up, I sat and leaned my weary back against the rough wall of the shed and rested my head in my hands, scarcely aware of the tears slicking my cheeks.

That was how Terrac found me. Unconsciously, I sensed his approach, even before I felt his hands gripping me firmly by the shoulders and raising me to my feet. I didn't bother to resist.

"You can't sit here crying," he said. "The fire has spread to the barn and the Fists are distracted. If we're ever going to escape, this is our chance. Get up."

Ordinarily, I would have been angry at his ordering me around, but I was empty of any emotion now, except pain. What did anything matter anymore, when things could never be right again?

I didn't realize I was sobbing until Terrac snapped, "Be quiet. There'll be time for grieving later. But for now, you have to do what I tell you or we'll never get out of this alive."

I obeyed and stopped my bawling, only because it felt like too much trouble to argue. I allowed him to lead me to the onion cart, where he told me to stand at the horse's head and keep hold of the bridle.

"Don't move until I return," he ordered and he left me there. He disappeared around the shed and returned a few minutes later, dragging Brig's lifeless body along behind him. I kept my eyes forward but listened to the muffled grunts and sounds of him struggling to lift the heavy corpse into the back of the cart. He didn't ask for my help, which was good because I didn't know that I was in a condition to give any. Lost inside my own wretched world, nothing of what occurred in this one seemed of any significance.

There was a heavy thud as Terrac achieved his goal and then he was beside me again, snatching the horse's halter and leading the animal forward. I shuffled alongside the cart, because I knew he would prod me if I didn't, and we moved away from the hold yard with its crackling blaze and out into the night. Terrac never tried urging the horse to speed, but gently coaxed the nervous animal every step of the way. We moved with nothing like stealth as we lurched along with our creaking, rickety cart and in a different time, I would have been amused by our pathetic retreat.

But, despite our clumsy flight, no enemy shouted or came running in pursuit as we put distance behind us. Terrac kept us well away from the road and we slogged our way along over uneven, rocky terrain. I decided my throbbing ribs weren't broken as I'd first supposed, but walking was still little short of agony. It was only sheer willpower pushing me forward and that will was more Terrac's than mine.

The rain made our journey doubly miserable and even when it abated, it left behind a deep clingy mud, making walking difficult. Twice, the wheels of our cart sunk into the mud and it took both of us pushing to break free again. Slowly, I came back to myself a little. After the second halt to free the cart from a mud sink, I broke the long silence between us.

"So how did you escape?" I asked the question because it seemed I should, not because I truly cared to know. "The last I saw of you, you were being dragged into the house by a handful of Fists. I didn't think you'd get free of them alive."

"I'm glad to know you considered that when you sent me in," Terrac said coldly. "It took me some time to realize this was how you planned things all along. That you fed me to the wolves intentionally."

"I didn't do it for myself, if that makes any difference to you."

"It doesn't."

"It wasn't personal, Terrac. It was for Brig. I had to give you up."

"Yes, I know," he said. "Don't think I didn't see your reasoning or feel its implications. You put Brig's rescue ahead of the safety of the 'cowardly boy priest' because you believed his wellbeing was the more important of the two. His is the life of value."

"Was," I interjected miserably, but he appeared

not to hear me.

"I thought we were friends, Ilan, but I should have known better than to trust someone like you."

"Yes, maybe you should have," I snapped. "Maybe this friendship should never have begun. What common ground could there be between a worthless woods thief and a high-minded priest-in-training? Does it occur to you for a moment that if you had been different, I might have put your life first? But it's difficult to care about someone who doesn't stand up for himself or anyone else, who never shows a sliver of courage or confidence when you need it."

I sensed I hurt him, even if he didn't show it. A long silence stretched and when he spoke again, his voice was emotionless. "I bumped a log from the fireplace when no one was watching and caught the floor rushes afire. They were so dry they went up like kindling, and I slipped out during the confusion."

It took me a moment to remember what he was talking about. "And what did you tell them, that they allowed you to sit unwatched and unbound?"

"Exactly what you told me to say, that I was a good priest and an honest man. Your words came back to me when they questioned me, as I suppose you intended them to. I invented a story of how I was traveling late along the road when the storm blew up and upon seeing the light in the window of the hold house, decided to stop and beg shelter for the evening. I approached stealthily at first because the place had an abandoned look and I feared I would stumble upon thieves or other dangerous folk trespassing."

He shrugged and added, "The Fists said I had too 'soft' a look about me to be a cutthroat and besides, I had the mark of the church to lend credence to my story."

He indicated the pale scar of the priesthood branded on the inside of his forearm.

"So they decided I was harmless," he said. "I was permitted to share their fire and what food they had, which was decent of them. They didn't seem like bad men."

"Oh no, not bad men at all," I said sarcastically. "They'll sit down to share a bit of bread with a stranger and they've got pretty shiny armor and better polished manners. But what they did to Brig, oh, that was purely incidental."

He frowned. "I'm not saying they were right in the way they treated him, but let us remember Brig was an outlaw and well aware of the penalties he would face—"

"Penalties?" I broke in, unable to contain my anger. "*Penalties!* Did you see what they did to him? Stop the cart! Walk back there and take a look."

"I didn't mean—" he tried to say, but I wouldn't be soothed.

"I said take a look! I want you to see, to know what your 'decent' heroes did to him."

I could feel the tendons standing out on my

neck and the hot blood rushing to my face, but I didn't care. I suddenly realized I needed to smash something. Anything. Terrac's face would do.

But he didn't give me an excuse. Drawing a deep breath as if to steady his emotions, he said, "I think we'd best speak no more on this. We're both weary and at the end of our tethers, and further discussion will only lead to more hasty words and later, to regrets."

I said, "I'm in the mood for hasty words and regrets and I'll speak on as I please."

"Then I refuse to stay and listen."

He quickened his pace to move ahead of me, effectively ending our discussion, for I couldn't muster the stamina to keep up. I suspected he knew my aching ribs made quick strides a torment.

We kept up our forward progress, passing along the edge of a shallow wooded ravine sometime late in the night. I was lost deep in my dark broodings so that I didn't immediately notice when one wheel of the cart got too near the edge and began to slide in the mud toward the downside of the gap. Not until I saw the cart tilt sharply sideways did I realize it was about to fall.

"Terrac!" I shouted. "The cart!"

But it was too late. The rickety cart skidded further in the muddy earth and Terrac dove out of its path no more than a second before the entire cart flipped over and tumbled down the hillside, dragging the struggling horse after it. I stood rooted to the spot as both cart and horse disappeared into the darkness below. I could hear the rig crashing through the trees on the way down, the awful screams of the horse plunging helplessly after it, and finally the thud as they hit bottom.

I didn't wait for more than that. Ignoring the pain in my side, I threw myself recklessly over the steep edge and began scrambling down the hillside. I heard Terrac clambering after me, but as he paused to pick his way more cautiously than I did, I reached the bottom before him. I first discovered Brig's body, thrown from the cart. Nearby, the gray horse was tangled in its harness and half-buried beneath the rig, but still alive and screaming shrilly as it thrashed to free itself from beneath the wreckage. Its movements gradually quieted, growing feebler as I approached and I saw at a glance it wouldn't survive.

I heard the noisy approach of Terrac behind me and left him to put the animal out of its misery. I could handle only so many gruesome tasks in a night. I turned my back on the scene and tried not to be aware of what happened, which was difficult because Terrac had to interrupt my unawareness twice, once to request the use of my knife and again to inquire where he ought to place the blade for the swiftest result.

The cart, I determined next, was beyond repair. Both wheels were shattered, not that that particularly mattered with no way to bring it out of the ravine and no horse to pull it even if we could accomplish that feat. I climbed back up the hillside, collecting as many scattered pieces of the rig as I could find, and heaping them into a pile. Terrac helped me lift Brig's remains gently onto the top of the heap. Then the priest boy wisely withdrew to a copse of pines on the far side of the hill, leaving me alone with my grievous task.

I gathered an armful of brush, the driest I could find on such a damp night, piling it carefully around the body, and removed my ragged old cloak, using it to cover Brig's face. For lack of a better parting gift, I laid one of my long-bladed knives across his chest. I remembered the strange bow I still carried and briefly considered leaving it instead, but somehow I was reluctant to part with it. Anyway, it hardly made a fitting gift either. There seemed nothing more to be done and so I used my flint stone to set fire to the smaller bits of brush, managing after several tries to coax to life a fitful flame. The fire spread reluctantly over the rain-dampened kindling, but at length, the entire funeral pyre was wreathed in flames.

I sat at the edge of the circle of firelight that penetrated the night and watched the blaze consume Brig. Whenever the flames threatened to die, I added more brush until I had a tall bonfire raging. The heat warmed my face and the smoke burned my eyes, but I didn't move back. After a time, I reached behind me and, for no particular reason, pulled out the bow to examine.

It was a finely crafted weapon, making it all the stranger that I discovered it in an abandoned barn. The pale wood looked and smelled freshly cut and took on an almost living glow beneath the firelight. It took me a moment to realize the carvings spiraling up the limb weren't random designs, but strange runes unlike anything I'd ever seen. I had a peculiar feeling, looking at those runes, almost like the stirring of magic I felt when sensing another life nearby. Maybe I would ask Terrac later if he could decipher the unfamiliar form of writing. He was the scholar, not me.

But hard on the heels of that thought came the memory that the priest boy and I weren't exactly on friendly terms at the moment. I glanced at the burning pyre and loneliness washed over me as I remembered the one person who cared for me most, the only friend who knew about my forbidden talents, was now gone forever. In the face of that, everything else lost significance. When I looked back to the bow, there appeared to be a forlorn sense to its unreadable runes that matched my pain.

It was a mark of the strangeness of my mood that I didn't flinch this time when the bow began to glow orange and gold. I felt it grow warm in my hands and pulse like a stilled heartbeat throbbing suddenly to life. Inside my head, I seemed to hear its quiet moans of anguish, perhaps echoing my hurt, or maybe crying out for some loss of its own. Either way, the result was oddly comforting. I continued tracing my fingers absently up and down the runes as I watched the flickering flames.

My grief grew muted and while there was a chill loneliness in my heart, an ache of regret beyond words, I shed no more tears for my loss. It was as if, with the death of Brig, my own essence had abandoned me as well, leaving me incapable of feeling anything but emptiness. Was this how Rideon had grown so cold? I felt a sudden surge of understanding for the man, an understanding that had nothing to do with sympathy or affection.

Trying to shake this alarming change, I dug deep inside myself seeking some spark to prove who I was still hid within, but it was like reaching into an empty shell. I dipped into a chasm of nothingness, sifting blank thoughts and meaningless images through my fingers in search of something I knew should be there. Even my unease at this discovery was a quiet, distant thing as if I were merely a witness, observing myself through another's eyes.

I felt older, emptier, and vastly changed as I sat hunched before the flames, lost in thought, until the fire burned low and a pale dawn came to chase away the stars.

CHAPTER FOURTEEN

I WATCHED TERRAC WARILY THE FOLLOWING morning, but if he was still angry over my betraying him to the Fists, he gave no sign of it. It took us all of the following day to find our way to the place in the wood where the trees never greened. Here, the rest of our band had set up a temporary camp after evacuating Molehill and Red Rock. It was nearly dark by the time we stumbled on the outlaws a few miles upstream of the creek leading to Red Rock falls. The gathering was large, the combined number of both our camps crowded together into the temporary one.

Immediately on arrival, I felt a pervading sense of gloom hanging in the air. Until now, we thought ourselves impervious to attack, hidden as we were deep within the safety of Dimming's shadows. But our confidence had been shaken and we were all acutely aware of the danger that might break over our heads at any time. No one knew as yet what had become of our homes at Red Rock and Molehill; the only thing we could be certain of was that it was unsafe to return. Rideon moved among the outlaws, planning with them, seeking to lift their confidence. Wherever he had been, spirits lifted, but it was obvious it would take time for us to recover our former self-assurance.

I had to give an explanation for my disappearance and as my story quickly spread through the gathering, I was hailed as a kind of hero. No one appeared to care that I had set out to save Brig and returned without him. What mattered was that one of their own had struck a blow back at the Praetor's men. A dozen times over, my attack on the Fists was declared the most daring and bold deed anyone had ever heard of from such a youngster. Suddenly, men who hadn't so much as given me their names before today were clapping me on the back and congratulating me around the campfire.

Terrac, unwilling to partake in the glory, wandered off and left me to deal with it alone. In a different time I would have enjoyed retelling my tale as many times as it was requested and recounting my actions in the most fantastically exaggerated manner possible. But now I couldn't enjoy the attention because I knew, whatever the others thought, my mission was a failure.

My thoughts were dark ones that first night back, as I sat surrounded by my throng of newfound admirers. I huddled over a bowl of venison stew, not because I was hungry, but because someone had shoved it into my hands. I forced the warm liquid down my throat, reasoning that as long as I kept my mouth full, I couldn't be expected to talk. I was quickly wearying of recounting my adventure.

When I heard the sounds of someone's approach and silence descended over my companions, I didn't need to look up to know Rideon stood over me. I was expecting this moment.

"Hound," Rideon greeted me.

I knew now was the time to apologize and beg forgiveness for disobeying his orders in following Brig, but I couldn't find enough fear inside to prod me to it. Instead, I looked up and met his gaze unflinchingly.

He didn't react with the anger I expected.

"The men tell me you are a hero tonight, that you've defeated a handful of the Praetor's Fists and survived to boast of it. They also say you've killed the traitor Resid."

"I did," I admitted, bracing myself for whatever was coming.

"Perhaps I've underestimated your courage and skill. You broke my orders, but in so doing, you risked your life to strike a blow for all of us. For that, it seems to be the general will we should honor you tonight. Bold deeds notwithstanding, I warn you the next time you discount a command of mine so blatantly I'll kill you on the spot." Here his voice hardened momentarily. "But on this singular occasion, it would be ungrateful to kill a returning hero."

He offered the ghost of a smile or the nearest thing to one I had ever seen on his face. "And so, for this night and this night alone, I make you immune to our laws. Revel in your glory for a few hours and at dawn return to work."

He looked around at the gathered assembly. "All of us will set to work. There are difficult days ahead, but I'm confident we will survive this setback and be the stronger for it."

As he turned on his heel and strode away, I wished I could feel flattered, could know a thrill of joy at receiving this recognition before my comrades. But the time when I would have felt pleased was past. I didn't know what I wanted anymore.

Despite Rideon's advice to enjoy the moment, I sought my bed early that night. I was exhausted and the purple bruises marring my ribs still pained me. I found an out of the way spot, well distanced from the others, and curled up beneath a tall elder tree.

I woke at one point during the night, thinking I heard footsteps rustling in the leaves nearby and Terrac softly calling my name. I kept still and when his footsteps eventually receded, breathed a sigh of relief. I didn't know why he sought me, but all I wanted was to be left alone tonight. I cradled my head in one arm and rested my other hand on the finely grained wood of the bow beside me. I didn't have any arrows for it as yet. I thought in the morning I would ask Dradac to make me some fine new ones, the best he ever fletched. I fell asleep stroking the smooth wood and vaguely wondering that it felt warm to my touch.

Despite my exhaustion, I spent a troubled night

tossing and turning on the rocky ground. For the first time in a long while I dreamed of the night my mother died all those years ago and of the brooch she left me. Then I dreamed of Hadrian, the priest of Light who promised to teach me about magic if I came to him in Selbius.

I awoke early the next morning and lay awake, staring up into the scattered patches of lightening sky peeking between the leafless branches of the trees overhead. I was unused to seeing so much sky. The bare branches made it look later in the season than it was, but I knew elsewhere in the forest the trees would still be thick with greenery. Three days short of Middlefest, it seemed wrong to be surrounded by this gloom and deadness.

I rose and passed through camp, stepping carefully to avoid trampling on the sleeping forms of my comrades where they huddled on the ground. I remembered from past explorations a small spring not far from this spot, probably one of the factors Rideon had taken into account when settling on this site. Finding the gurgling stream only a little distance away, I knelt and washed the sleep from my eyes and filled my waterskin.

When I rose from the stony banks, I found Brig sitting nearby on a fallen log, watching me. His grey eyes were fixed on a point in the distance, his weathered face creased in the half-frown that always meant he was puzzling over something. He rubbed listlessly at the calluses on his rough hands and his mouth moved, as if he were muttering beneath his breath. The sight of him sent a pang through me, but I felt no shock or alarm, only comfort. I shook my head and smiled, noting how the front of his faded woolen tunic was fastened crookedly. I leaned forward to right it for him, as I had done many times before, and stopped abruptly, my hands hovering inches from him.

Cold reason reasserted itself and Brig's image wavered. I had to stop this. Brig was gone. Unless I wished to let go of my reason entirely and live the rest of my life in a world of pathetic imaginings, a place where the dead walked and events I didn't like could be changed, I needed to pull back from what I was doing. As much as it pained me to do it, I pushed Brig's flickering image aside and forced myself to see the reality instead. The space opposite me was empty, occupied only by a fallen tree stump with a handful of jumper beetles crawling on its surface.

But my vision of Brig helped me form a decision I'd been contemplating for a long time. It was as if he had appeared to remind me of things I already knew but had refused until now to accept. Of old obligations unfulfilled and promises broken.

I returned to camp, where the outlaws were just beginning to stir in their dew-soaked blankets. Someone started to build a campfire, until Rideon ordered there be no fires lit today. We weren't safe from discovery yet, he said.

I slipped quietly among the men, found the lonely spot where I had passed the night, and collected my bow. Then I set my back to the camp and my comrades without a word of farewell. No one called out to me or even, I suspected, noted my departure.

I'd come to a decision and with this new-found direction a little of the strangeness of last night fell away. I was done settling for whatever fate served up to me. If I followed along the road life set at my feet the future was already a given. I would be a hunted criminal, forced to skulk within the boundaries of Dimming the rest of my life, wondering daily if this would be the day a Fist's blade or the Praetor's noose found me. Such an existence I had once craved but Brig's death had opened my eyes to the waste of it.

It was time to step off that path.

NOT AN ENDING, BUT
A RESTING PLACE

G OLDEN AND AMBER LEAVES CRUNCH loudly beneath my boots, startling my thoughts back to the present, as I follow the forest trail leading away from Rideon and the others. I have come far since the dark night so long ago when I lost my parents. In some ways I've journeyed farther still since losing Brig two nights ago. But as I leave the outlaw camp behind, anticipation stirs within me and I contemplate the distance I have yet to travel.

A sudden flair of warmth radiating from the bow slung across my back seems to echo my sense of hope.

ABOUT THE AUTHOR

C. Greenwood is the fantasy pen name of author Dara England, who lives in Oklahoma with her husband, two young children, and a Yorkshire terrier. To receive updates on future books, visit www.DaraEnglandAuthor.com and sign up for her monthly newsletter.

WRITING AS C. GREENWOOD
Legends of Dimmingwood Series
Magic of Thieves ~ Book I
Betrayal of Thieves ~ Book II
Circle of Thieves ~ Book III
Redemption of Thieves ~ Book IV

Other Titles
Dreamer's Journey

WRITING AS DARA ENGLAND
The Accomplished Mysteries
Accomplished in Murder ~ Book One
Accomplished in Detection ~ Book Two
Accomplished in Blood ~ Book Three

The American Heiress Mysteries
Death on Dartmoor ~ Book One
Murder in Mayfair ~ Book Two

Other Titles
Beastly Beautiful
Love By The Book
The Magic Touch
Eternal Strife (The Mammoth
Book of Irish Romance)

Made in the USA
Lexington, KY
22 March 2014